This was … just a kiss or a few copped feels. She'd make sure of it....

"Are you okay?" her cowboy asked, dipping to nip at her neck.

Was he asking if Lucy was going to regret this? Hardly. "Just keep doing what you're doing," she instructed, getting more turned on by the moment.

But then suddenly he did something she didn't expect: he kissed her, a gentle touch of his mouth to hers. No rough insistence. No animal passion.

This wasn't what Lucy expected from a one-night stand. It was too intimate, which was ironic considering what had happened so far. Out of a sense of self-preservation, Lucy reached down to his crotch. Rigid, big... She wanted him inside her, that was all. Wanted to know what it would be like to enjoy pure physical pleasure with no momentous expectations attached. "I just want it...naughty, okay?"

And then she got her wish. He made a strangled noise low in his throat and, before she knew what was happening, he'd brought her flush against him, devouring her with his lips, feverishly pulling off her clothes. *Yes!* she thought, finally tasting what she was so hungry for. Naughty was *definitely* the way to go....

ROMANCE

Dear Reader,

A few years ago a friend and I took a trip down part of Route 66. (You all know Sheri WhiteFeather!) I had a story idea for a chick-lit book, so off we went, zooming down the Mother Road.

While my chick-lit story never came to fruition, I kept all my notes from visiting places like Lake Havasu, Oatman and Grand Canyon Caverns, among all the other strange and barren places on the route. Someday, I thought, I was going to write a Route 66 story.

I just never realized it would be a Harlequin Blaze book.

I hope you get to discover this wonderful road one day. But in the meantime, if you visit my Web site at www.crystal-green.com, you can see a few pictures from our trip. I hope it conjures up some dreams and lends another element to this story about strangers who become much more than just one-night stands....

Enjoy!

Crystal Green

ONE FOR THE ROAD

Crystal Green

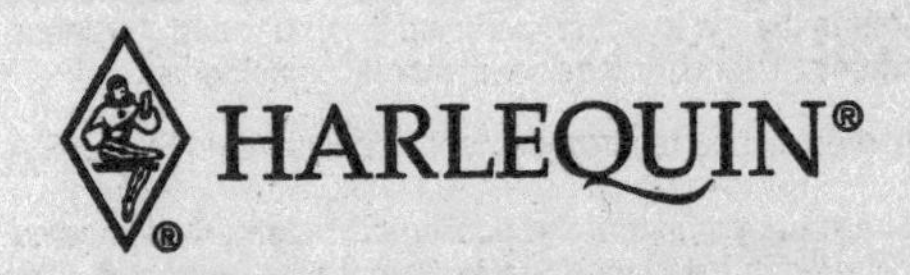

TORONTO • NEW YORK • LONDON
AMSTERDAM • PARIS • SYDNEY • HAMBURG
STOCKHOLM • ATHENS • TOKYO • MILAN • MADRID
PRAGUE • WARSAW • BUDAPEST • AUCKLAND

ISBN-13: 978-0-373-79391-4
ISBN-10: 0-373-79391-X

ONE FOR THE ROAD

This edition published by arrangement with Harlequin Books S.A.

www.eHarlequin.com

Printed in U.S.A.

ABOUT THE AUTHOR

Crystal Green lives near Las Vegas, Nevada, where she writes Harlequin Blaze, Silhouette Special Edition and vampire tales. She loves to read, overanalyze movies, practice yoga, travel and detail her obsessions on her Web site, www.crystal-green.com. You can even see a few pictures of her trip on Route 66, where she didn't get into half the trouble Lucy and Carmen find....

Books by Crystal Green

HARLEQUIN BLAZE

121—PLAYMATES
179—BORN TO BE BAD
261—INNUENDO
303—JINXED!
"Tall, Dark & Temporary"
334—THE ULTIMATE BITE

SILHOUETTE SPECIAL EDITION

1574—HER MONTANA MILLIONAIRE
1587—THE BLACK SHEEP HEIR
1668—THE MILLIONAIRE'S SECRET BABY
1670—A TYCOON IN TEXAS
1724—PAST IMPERFECT
1752—THE LAST COWBOY
1838—THE PLAYBOY TAKES A WIFE

Stacy, thank you for your continued support.
Here's to having found love on the road,
even if it wasn't necessarily the first stop.

1

IT WAS JUST a few days before Lucy Christie's thirtieth birthday when she finally had *the* epiphany.

"This is my life," she said to her traveling companion Carmen. They were both sitting in a roadside diner, Lucy staring at the detailed travel itinerary she'd formulated. "Point A to point B in a certain window of time. No deviations, every moment laid out to the minute."

She glanced up to find her best friend putting down her digital camera and studying her. And why not? Only seconds before, Carmen had been aiming her lens at a framed poster of Marilyn Monroe amidst the clutter of a memorabilia-filled wall, and they'd both been bopping in their booth to a Petula Clark song. Now, it was suddenly all about Lucy's Major Life Crisis.

The epiphany still made her head feel like a gong that'd been rung. "I was looking at travel day five, and I realized I've suspected the truth all along. I've had my hours, my months, my *years* planned out since I was old enough to make lists. I'm boring, Carm, and that's only one reason Greg broke up with me. That's why they *all* have. I'm boring, I have impossible expectations for my relationships and I'm so afraid of not reaching them that I've become Needy Woman."

"You're nothing of the sort."

But Lucy knew it was true. Greg's parting words to her kept vibrating her eardrums, even now, three months later.

"I feel like we've already been married for seven years," he'd said, "and we've been going out for only four months."

On that note, she'd let him go, too pained to ask for more of an explanation. She didn't need one. All she'd ever wanted was to have a happy family—kisses in the morning, two cars in the garage, a swing set in the backyard—just like her parents had provided. But when had she started putting such pressure on her boyfriends to get it?

When had she started becoming so afraid that she never would?

Carmen sent Lucy a sympathetic glance. "You're freaking out because you're turning the big three-oh. That's all. I went through it, too, Luce."

A confident smile tilted Carmen's red-lipstick mouth as she relaxed against the back of her seat, one bare arm riding the top of it.

There'd never been a lack of confidence with her, Lucy thought. Then again, Carmen Ferris, with her punky tank top advertising a garage band, her red-tinted hair layered in saucy abandon down to her ears and the glint sparkling in her gold eyes, had never done self-esteem issues. Not even in college at San Diego State, when Lucy had met her in a lower-level business administration course. Lucy had considered herself so very serious and a bit mousy, but Carmen had had no tolerance for that, telling her classmate to get over herself and come to a dorm party with her that night.

Now, Carmen continued, aiming her camera around a room choked with the aroma of grilled meat and fries. "Two weeks of utter brainless joy in Vegas and then it's on to the road. We came on this vacation to have some good prebirthday fun, get away from the grind of work and cheer you up after the Greg thing."

The breakup, Lucy thought. The latest kiss-off, just another link in her chain of failed romances—none of which had lasted beyond the four months she'd spent with Greg. Maybe this one had left her reeling extra hard because it'd been a record for how long a guy had stuck with her.

Carmen was escaping the aftermath of a breakup, as well, but she'd been dating her now-ex-boyfriend for years. Aeons, as far as Lucy was concerned.

Glancing back at the itinerary, she sighed. She had planned their time to a T, charmed by all the guidebook descriptions of Route 66, where they could see the mythos of the West disappearing into the sunset and eat at a string of greasy spoons while witnessing the kitsch of a more romantic time. Just scanning her schedule, each stop didn't seem like an adventure so much as a future accomplishment, an item to check off a master list—exactly like the one she'd silently kept with every boyfriend.

With care, she tucked the itinerary into a leather folder. There. She hadn't exactly ripped it to shreds and let it fly away, but it was gone. After all, wasn't that the purpose of this trip? To liberate themselves from what was weighing them down back home?

It was supposed to be a trip that could make a girl like Carmen forget about going back to planning conventions in her cubicle back at the office, where she actually misspent most of her day flitting about the Internet and updating a blog that she said needed more spice. And maybe their jaunt could even take Lucy's mind off all those rules she had to deal with on a daily basis. As a human resources specialist for Padme

Software, she had been comfortably steeped in manuals and dos and don'ts for a few years now. However, she'd evidently been applying rigid standards to her relationships, too, without even realizing it.

Their waitress, decked out in a pink-and-aqua uniform, checked to see how they were doing with their meal. After smiling in approval and refusing to count all the calories she'd already consumed, Lucy glanced around Peggy Sue's 50's Diner. It was a cluttered lunchtime homecoming of truckers, locals and faded golden-age movie stars captured in photographs.

She breathed in the grease-thickened air and relaxed. Ah, the romance of life on the road. See? Better. Not freaked out anymore about being thirty or as boring as static on a TV screen at 3:00 a.m.

Or maybe she still was that old Lucy. But…why? Couldn't she truly leave the other woman behind just to see what it felt like to have no stringent goals or expectations?

Scanning farther, her gaze brushed over a table full of obvious tourists, then a couple whose body language indicated that they were in a fight.

Moving on.

Lucy's attempt to stop and smell the roses or burger patties or whatever continued, past the couple, into a back room where a cowboy sat in a darkened corner, his hat pulled low over his brow.

Her investigation came to a halt, although she couldn't say why.

Maybe it was because he fit in with her idealized notion of what a gritty Western sojourn should be. Shadow covered most of his face, but she could still discern a hint of pale eyes and stubble. Hunched over an emptied plate, he wore a T-shirt, faded jeans and boots like a careless attitude.

Broad-shouldered, big, muscled...

As something melted from her chest downward, Lucy realized that she was watching him.

And that he was watching her right back.

A bolt of fear—or excitement?—split through her, zapping straight down to her belly, then lower, where it settled into a churning, charged pool.

She held her breath, shocked by the sudden stiff ache that had settled between her legs.

She'd had sex before, but only when she and her boyfriends had a commitment, which usually happened in month one. By month two, they would have found a groove—nothing explosive in bed, but...nice. Just vanilla, dependable *nice.*

But this?

This wasn't...nice.

Turning back to her Mickey Mouse Club Sandwich, she tried to act as if she hadn't really noticed the stranger. That she hadn't been rattled by all the primal cells in her body finally waking up because they were excited about being away from home.

She shifted in her seat, and the ache only intensified. She felt herself going damp and excited by the thrill of being singled out.

Maybe she should just eat her food and ignore what her body was doing. That's why they'd come into this diner, right? They were still scheduled to visit Calico Ghost Town before checking into the MGM Hotel later. No time for detours.

Or maybe there should be.

As her epiphany rang through her head once more, she tried to chase it away by sipping from her cherry shake.

Then again, all she wanted to do was glance back at the cowboy, encouraging the slight throb of her sex until it became something bigger.

Was he was still watching her?

Just as she felt herself losing the battle to not look, a burst of noise sounded from the dining room's entrance. Both Lucy and Carmen turned to find a group of seven college-age kids plopping into a nearby booth. Carmen put down her bite of chicken-fried steak and followed them with her interested gaze.

Meanwhile, one of the spring-breakers eyed Carmen, too. Tall, with a flop of sandy hair nearly covering his green eyes. A devilish grin. Definitely Carm's type in that respect, at least.

Lucy cleared her throat loudly and ate a French fry while the new group got settled with their laminated menus.

"What?" Carmen asked, all innocence after she turned back to Lucy. "A girl can't look?"

Lucy laughed. "Cradle robbing. You know he was probably in second grade when you entered high school?"

"Well, just suck the fantasy right out of my head, why don't you." Carmen went back to her meal, but not before she grabbed her camera again and thought to photograph the half-eaten down-home dish. This vacation was great fodder for her blog. "Here I am, prepared to have a good post-bye-bye-boyfriend time and you put me on the straight and narrow."

The back of Lucy's neck tingled, sending shivers over her skin. The cowboy was looking, wasn't he?

Don't look back, she thought, even though she was dying to.

"Someone's got to be your chaperone," Lucy said. "Your family will thank me. Believe it."

"*Ay,*" Carmen said in exasperation. Her father was from the North, Anglo as could be with no old-country traditions to speak of. But her Mexican-American mother? *So* traditional. One look at Carmen's four married-with-children sisters showed exactly what was expected of the only single sibling left.

"As if I'd ever give in to Mama's begging and go back to Mal," Carmen added, using the nickname Lucy had recently given the man Carmen had been dating since college. *Ex*-boyfriend. Mal Odorous or Malcolm Ortega, as he was known in better days. Even if he'd blown it with Carmen by practicing his machismo on other women a couple months back, traditional Mama still adored him because Carmen hadn't told her what Malcolm had done yet. It would break Mama's heart to know that the perfect husband for her eldest daughter wasn't so great, and Carmen was dreading having to share the news.

Hence, yet another reason for this little trip to the desert. It was also supposed to give Carmen leeway to figure out a way to tell the family that Malcolm was permanently out of the picture, even if they still considered him a part of the brood in the hopes that she would come to her senses.

But Lucy knew that Carmen was merely procrastinating.

"Maybe you shouldn't have told the family that you wanted a couple of weeks to think about getting back together with Mal," Lucy said. "You gave them hope when you knew darned well that there isn't any."

"I just need time away to think about how I'm going to handle all the changes that this breakup brings, Luce. Besides, Malcolm begged me not to tell Mama exactly why we called it quits because he's afraid of Mama's disappointment, which we know she wields so well. He's trying to avoid the big moment of revelation just as much as I am. But for some reason, he seems to think I'm going to change my mind and everything will go back to the way it was, even though I've told him it won't happen. Not in a million years."

"You realize Mama's going to pursue what she wants like a bulldog until you come up with a better explanation than 'Me and Malcolm just grew apart.'"

"I know, I know, but…"

"But the thought of disappointing her is killing you, too." Lucy emphatically pointed at her friend. "You've always been her baby, and you never want to let her down. I know you too well."

"Do you?" Carmen raised a brow, then turned right around and focused her camera on the college crowd, who was whooping it up at their table.

Lucy noted that Carmen's favorite group member had caught her taking the picture of him. Good-naturedly, he grinned and jerked his chin in her direction, a sexy acknowledgment.

When she turned back around, she flapped a hand in front of her face. "Is it burning up in this place or what?"

Oh, great. Here, Lucy had just been starting to forget about the cowboy and…

Whooooosh…

A flare of heat waved over her as she thought about him in that shaded corner.

Unable to stop herself, she sneaked a glance to where she'd last seen the pale-eyed man brooding at his table.

But it was empty now.

Lucy didn't know why, but her veins seemed to tap out, going empty with…disappointment?

Heck, she thought. She didn't know how to flirt anyway. Nope, she usually skipped right over the fun stuff and straight to "serious." But maybe…

During this trip, could she figure out how to avoid that from now on? Could she follow in Carmen's more assured footsteps in her own attempt to recover and actually become her own woman?

Now she found her friend snapping another picture of the cute guy in the other booth. But this time he had his own camera aimed at *her.*

A professional-looking camera, too, from the looks of it.

As they both shutterbugged away, they laughed, and he got out of his seat to saunter over to them. His friends, both male and female, catcalled, but he waved them off.

"You got me," he said in a teasing voice as he came to stand at their table.

"And you got me right back," Carmen said, her eyes all but glowing with the intrigue of this little game.

Lucy's body was still afterburning from *her* thwarted bout of look-tag with the cowboy. But now it was Carmen's turn, and Lucy held back a smile as her friend went to work.

Watch and learn, she thought, already feeling as if she was leaving the sadder Lucy behind and becoming a little wiser.

All she had to do was get in the spirit of this trip.

"I'm Eddie," he said, holding out his free hand to Carmen.

In the background, one of his friends called out, "Edward, get back here, you dog."

Eddie cut the intruder off with a tolerant glare, but he was back to being adorable the next second, shrugging off the interruption and grinning at Carmen.

She introduced herself, and then Lucy.

Eddie sent Lucy a charming smile, addressing his next question to her, as if he didn't want to leave her out of whatever was going on. Thoughtful guy.

"You two headed to Vegas?"

Lucy placed her hand on her leather folder, reluctant to give out that information to someone who'd wandered over to their table from out of the blue. She might be willing to shed some of her old habits, but not her common sense.

Carmen obviously had a different interpretation of the circumstances. "Yes, we are. Three days of baking by the pool and losing lots of cash, then we're riding down part of Route 66."

"We are, too," Eddie said. "I mean, we're not going to Vegas, but we're taking our spring break to check out the old road." He held up his camera. "It's sort of a hobby of mine. Taking pictures. The Route is full of material. But some of the group might stay back at Lake Havisu while I move on. We'll see."

"Par-tay!" said an obviously eavesdropping girl from the group's booth, a blonde with curls and pink cheeks.

The rest of the crowd laughed and welcomed the waitress as she came to take their drink orders. Beers all around.

Carmen grabbed her pineapple shake and played with the straw. Lucy took note of the coquettish gesture because it looked as if it might work wonders.

"Spring break, huh?" her friend asked before taking a draw from her beverage.

Very subtly, Carmen was actually asking about his age, but either Eddie didn't catch that or he didn't care enough to comment. How old did he think *they* were?

"Spring break," he repeated. "And if you guys weren't intent on being high rollers, I'd invite you to the modest soiree we'll be having in our motel in Needles tonight. The Timberline Inn, just off Interstate 40."

When Carmen sent Lucy an interested glance, Lucy

widened her eyes. But…their itinerary? Surely they were going to keep to that.

If she was going to deviate, it wasn't going to be for some college party.

Lucy picked up the check that the waitress had already left and gestured that she was going to the cashier to pay up. Afterward, she figured she would linger in the gift shop she'd seen on the way in, allowing Carmen some amusement with young Eddie before they went on their way.

Yup, Carmen needed to get it out of her system, because there'd be a lot more Eddies in Vegas. And maybe Lucy would be up for that, too. Who could predict?

She told Carmen that she would either be in the gift shop or waiting in the car, thus setting a time limit for her friend's antics. Then she said a "good to meet you" to Eddie and sneaked off as their new friend slipped into the booth across from a delighted Carmen.

And, as Lucy walked past the table where the cowboy had been sitting, she wondered, ever so briefly, what might've happened if she had taken the risk of smiling at him as Carmen was smiling at Eddie.

If she had just taken that first fork in the road.

JOSHUA GRAY HAD NEVER considered himself invasive. Hell, he'd always kept pretty much to himself, had always taken great pleasure in lone nights on his ranch's porch with just the company of a good cigar. He'd even managed to stay out of any romantic entanglements, preferring to meet women during the business trips he used to take and then letting them go their own way once the night was done.

So why had he dawdled at the cashier's counter around the

corner from the main dining room, taking the time to listen to that kid inviting those women to a motel tonight?

He'd heard the whole exchange pretty well, all except for the part where they'd traded names.

Joshua had shaken himself out of his reluctant eavesdropping at that point. He had no business listening, and that discomfited him just as much as the party-with-a-college-pup invitation itself. So Joshua had forced himself to walk away, through a second, older booth-lined area and toward the exit.

The worst part? He knew damn well why he'd hung around to catch their conversation in the first place. It was the girl with the sable hair that waved to her shoulders, the one with eyes made true blue by a pair of slashing dark brows. The one with the full pink lips and the dimples that deepened when she laughed with her friend.

Lord knew what it was about her, but Joshua hadn't been able to look away as he'd lingered over cherry pie and coffee in his corner. Maybe it was her honeyed smile, or even the way she wore a spring dress.

Or maybe it was the urge to feel like a man again, and she seemed just the soft type to allow him that necessity. Losing most of his family's property in Fielding, Texas, tended to take away a guy's bluster.

But sex wasn't the initial reason he'd gone on the road. He needed to get his head on straight and to "cool his jets," as one of his two sisters might've said. Leaving the ranch for a while was supposed to help out with that—and it would hopefully give him enough temper-calming distance to formulate an airtight strategy for his return home.

Yup, he was out here to lick his wounds, but the arid loneliness of the desert was also buying time for a geological study of the land he still owned—the land their "family friend" Timothy Trent *hadn't* purchased when he'd so kindly "helped" them out by buying the rest of the ranch and saying he would sell it back when the Grays found enough money to manage it.

Trent's lie had been designed to hoodwink the Grays, since their seemingly affable neighbor knew damn well that they wouldn't be able to afford to buy the acreage back at the original selling price. Their *friend's* cost had gone way up since then, of course, and he had offered the excuse that he was a businessman with a bordering ranch. Nothing personal.

Joshua had been so naive. He had, as a matter of fact, been so desperate to bring the family horse-breeding facility back into the black after finding out how far his deceased father had run it into the ground that he'd trusted Trent.

Damn-fool thing to do.

But if there was oil on the land they still had…?

His blood rumbled as he recalled the seep he'd found while riding what was left of his property one day. Keeping the news to himself, Joshua had immediately gone to Trent, thinking he might soon have enough funds to secure his family's own land again, whether it was oil rich or not.

But *that's* when Trent had laid it all out for Joshua, revealing his betrayal and refusing to sell any of the land back.

Even without knowing about the oil.

In return, that's when Joshua had lost it with Trent, nearly attacking him. At that moment, he'd recognized a foreign violence and hatred within himself, and it was horrifying.

Fortunately, he'd left before giving in to it.

But now, with a cooler head earned from distance, Joshua wondered if the money from possible oil would provide him with enough cash to buy his family's land back from Trent. Or if their neighbor even deserved such civil treatment at all.

As he pushed that darkness away—it was just anger and frustration, not a real part of him at all, right?—he summoned the image, the fantasy of the dark-haired woman. For an instant, he actually felt that temper redirect its energy to his core, which heated and boiled with a new hunger.

Holding on to this reshaped sense of power rolling through him, he passed a gift shop with an ice-cream counter near the exit. Betty Boop, *Gone with the Wind, Wizard of Oz*—it housed every pop culture item imaginable. An Elvis figurine caught his eye and he couldn't pass it up. His younger sister Darianne loved the King, and she would light up at something like this.

After grabbing the item, he meandered around the store without rushing back to his truck. Displays of lunch boxes, hats, games, candy in plastic jars…they were a maze to him.

And, all the while, he knew he was stalling.

What for? Did he think he could get another glimpse of the brunette?

Did he think she would meet his glance again, but instead of shyly looking away this time, she might keep eye contact an inviting second longer?

Just as he brought the Elvis trinket to the counter, a tumble of awareness flashed down his entire body, and he knew.

She'd entered the shop.

When he glanced over, he saw that she had stopped to finger an Archie Comics apron.

His nethers stirred, caught by all the fantasies pumping through him like bad blood. He could imagine her locking gazes with him now, admitting that she'd followed him in here. He could picture her undoing the first button on her dress, then the second.

You want to feel good? she would ask in a sultry voice that had somehow kept its innocence. *You want to forget about what you're running from, all these miles away from home? Well, I can clear your mind, Joshua. I can make you feel valuable again.*

Yet when his vision cleared, he just saw a beautiful woman moving on to the candy rack, running her fingers over the jars of bubble gum and Tootsie Rolls.

Sweet, he thought. She'd probably taste so sweet to a bitter man.

But he wouldn't say a damn thing to her, not in the state he was in. He would move on, pay for his sister's gift, then leave this woman in peace—which is what he, himself, wished to find so far away from Fielding.

Trying to shut out the rage, the humiliation, of having his property—his everything—more or less stolen from him, Joshua paid for Elvis, then waited as the cashier wrapped up the figurine. Yet, bit by bit, red filtered over his gaze, building, thickening, until he clenched his fists in an effort to contain it.

Each sleepless night, his plans to get the Triple Oaks back crept up on him, but that didn't do anything to make him whole again. The only time something had taken the place of the emptiness was when he'd seen the brunette across the crowded dining room, wearing her simple dress, her soothing smile.

But, he thought as he thanked the cashier and tucked the bag under his arm, he knew this attraction had nothing to do with candied kisses and romance. For better or worse, sex had always gone a long way in bolstering his confidence. While growing up, he'd been known as a quiet bad boy, devoted to his family but never a steady girlfriend. That hadn't kept the girls from trying to break him though. In fact, women had come so easy for him that he'd started to take them for granted in college, then after, during business-trip flings.

But then his mom had passed, and he'd seen how much his dad missed love, and Joshua had realized there was something he could've been overlooking all this time.

Focused upon leaving—just leaving and finding his own way—he made for the shop's exit. He tried not to think about the brunette taking up with a random guy who had approached them in a diner, tried not to think about what might happen to a couple of women who didn't know any better than to avoid strangers on the long, hard road.

Yet the brunette had moved on to a display of *Star Wars* items, and she was blocking the nearest aisle.

Either he would have to take a shortcut and admit a certain defeat, or he would have to pass her to get out.

Resentment rose in his gorge. He wasn't about to deal with another loss, no matter how trivial.

As he forged ahead, nearer, so agonizingly nearer to her, she glanced up. It was as if she sensed him, *scented* him even, just as he had already inhaled her own soft smell from a few feet away.

Powdery, he thought, but with a primal tinge underneath it all, like pink hiding a layer of red.

When she focused on him, her eyes widened in recognition—one that told him he'd managed to affect her, whether good or bad. He came to a halt, unable to take another step.

His blood pounded, echoing in his ears, his chest.

His cock.

He nodded at her, tipped his hat, wishing he had it in him

to smile. Maybe that would chase away the suddenly fearful tint that had overtaken her blue gaze.

"I don't bite, ma'am," he said, voice gruffer than he'd meant.

She blinked, then laughed a little, as if she didn't know what else to do.

He'd affected her, all right, and damn it, the knowledge gave him that power he'd lost. Gave him back a fraction of his old fire, his old sense of self.

What would happen if he was inside of her, fully connected and electrified at the source? What would he feel *then?*

She stepped out of the aisle before he could even ask. "Didn't mean to block your way."

He should've passed her, but...her voice got to him. As light as dawn over the ranch, it summoned a twinge of times gone by, when the place had thrived back before his mom had died and his dad had stopped caring about everything else, even the home he'd shared with his true love.

But Joshua would get those times—his *land*—back, just as sure as he would set things to rights with Timothy Trent, even if it was the last thing he did.

"Not to worry," Joshua said. *Just go.*

But it wasn't happening. Hell, no, instead he was searching for something to say, something that would extend their interaction.

She glanced down at the trinket shelf again, just as quiet as she'd been when her pal had flirted with that college kid. When the guy had invited them to the Timberline Inn, off I-40.

Suddenly, Joshua was unable to stop himself from being invasive.

"I couldn't help overhearing you talking with that college kid back there," he said, pushing his Stetson back on his head.

"And I'm no doubt out of line, but... You'll want to be careful of overly friendly men out here."

She finally looked back up, eyes as clear as a calm sky. Then, as if she'd had to think about doing it, she smiled at him.

Something tugged at his gut—sexual, deep...even protective. But Joshua nudged that last feeling aside in favor of the others.

"There're those who'd prey on two women by themselves," he added.

Her pink lips parted, as if in reaction to his warning. Little did she know that he was the stranger she should be most worried about.

"Thanks..." she said. "I mean, it's nice of you to take the time to tell me that. We're trying to be alert."

Then why are you standing here still talking to me? he wanted to ask.

As he searched for more to say, she took a deep breath, then seemed to allow a mildly amused grin to take over her mouth. He didn't think she was wearing lipstick; it looked as if she'd just finished sucking on berries during a lazy afternoon.

His groin tightened again and he took his bag from under his arm and repositioned it over his jeans.

"The Timberline's not a bad place, mind you," he finally managed to say. "I'm staying there myself."

A pulse of interest seemed to fill her gaze. "So it's the company I should be thinking about, not the motel itself. Right? It's a safe spot?"

"I only picked the Timberline out of a need for a bed to rest in tonight, but from what the truckers say, it's clean and well run."

She seemed to turn that over in her mind, but the speculative spark remained behind. "Well then, thanks again. We weren't planning on going there anyway, but it's good to know."

"No problem, ma'am."

"Ma'am," she said under her breath.

She paused. Then her smile changed tone—and hell if he couldn't understand just what had happened in front of his very eyes. Had she gone from merely being friendly to something more?

"Do you know the damage you can do to a woman of my age with those 'ma'am's'?" she asked.

Yup, something had definitely clicked up another level here.

"Miss, then?" he asked, realizing that he should've already wondered about whether or not she was significantly attached to anyone.

Or maybe he shouldn't be thinking about that.

Yet his body disagreed. In spite of all his misgivings, he found himself leaning toward her, bracing an arm on the wall next to him. The action brought him that much closer to her—a reach away.

Maybe he imagined it, but he thought he saw her run a slow glance over his arm, then his chest, before she made eye contact again. The subtle scan revved his libido.

Then, all too abruptly, she cleared her throat, as if chiding herself for some reason.

"Well," she said, "I ought to..."

She motioned toward the exit.

"I guess maybe you ought," he said, not moving a muscle, because he had the feeling she didn't really want to go anywhere, either.

Even if she didn't know it yet.

"Got a lot of road to cover today," she added.

Still, she didn't retreat.

He grabbed at one last straw. "Where are you off to?"

"Back to Interstate 15," she said evasively. "And you? I mean, after tonight?"

Nowhere, he thought. Just...away.

That hunger for fulfillment...for *something*...consumed him again, and he leaned closer to her.

"Would I-15 mean you're going to Vegas?" he asked.

A storm seemed to darken her eyes—a cloud-filled crossroads that he recognized because he'd reached it so many times himself these past few days.

Was she wondering if she should inch nearer to *him,* tell him the first bit of personal information about herself even though he had dodged her own question about his destination?

Yearning scorched Joshua, singeing every nerve ending until his skin screamed for her.

But then her gaze cleared, and she drew back ever so slightly, barely enough for a person not paying as much attention as he was to notice.

"Wherever *you're* going," she said, reaching behind her so she wouldn't knock over any shelves, "don't talk to those strangers yourself, now."

And, before she turned away and deserted him, he thought he saw her smile again—a hot, alluring invitation that burned away before he could really read it.

In the aftermath, Joshua Gray stood there, the name *Timberline Inn* echoing in his otherwise empty chest.

Calling to him like a disappeared dawn.

2

LUCY WENT STRAIGHT to the car, veins tangled from the encounter with the cowboy.

Point B, she thought, blood thudding in a cadence that connected her body in one neon throb. *I need to get to the next spot on the map before I accidentally go back in to that gift shop.*

After unlocking the driver-side door, she got behind the wheel, breathing deeply in an effort to gather herself.

He'd shaken her in an erotic way, as if she'd woken up from a crimson-hot dream, her heart stomping, her adrenaline running loose. Suddenly, in his unexpected presence, she'd become kind of flirtatious, actually giving him one of those smiles Carmen was so good at. One of those tacit invitations that might've told the cowboy that it was okay for him to reach over and touch her.

Lucy rubbed her goose-bumped arms. She wasn't used to stepping out of her shell at first, but obviously a more aggressive man did it for her. Her usual game consisted of being caught after some modest wooing, then ended with *her* chasing a guy who'd already won her over.

But the cowboy, with his silvered eyes and bad-boy stubble, seemed saturated in the possibility of a darker temptation, and she didn't need that to mess her up after the latest heartbreak.

Or…did she?

What if she could be a woman who wasn't a straitlaced, goal-driven myopic? Would she actually find fulfillment in some freedom?

She reclined against the headrest, conjuring him up again until her flesh went hot. His lips on hers, his stubble burning her cheeks, his fingers toying with her breasts. Then, in her fantasy, she guided his hand down to where she really wanted it—between her legs to stroke her…

As the noon sun sprayed through the windshield, she shoved the images away, straightening in her seat and fumbling with her CD cases until she chose a music mix.

Still, the fantasy remained alive, as if it'd finally been unleashed. She turned on the stereo so her Mellow Mix could sing through her and take her over.

Ben Harper, soulful and soft. Perfect.

But when Carmen opened the door and got into the passenger seat, the relaxing flow—the rhythm of repeated verses and chained notes—was broken.

"We're totally going to that motel tonight," Carmen said, a canary-eating grin on her face as she lowered the music's volume.

That motel—the one where the cowboy said he'd be staying, as well.

Lucy's carefully constructed day fractured ever so slightly, but then she remembered the lure of those MGM reservations. "We can't cancel in Vegas now. Not unless we want to pay for that room whether we're there or not. That might happen, you know."

"I'll fork over the cash, Luce. We don't have to be structured. It's vacation."

"I'm not thinking about the money so much as..." As what? Lucy put on her "mature face" and turned to Carmen. "You'd rather party with kids than relax in Vegas. *Vegas,* where we can go wine tasting at the Rio or see a Cirque du Soleil show."

"Pretty please?" Carmen playfully batted her eyelashes and smiled. "We live five hours by car from the place, and it's not going anywhere. But, I daresay, Eddie won't be waiting quite as long."

"Eddie. Yikes, Carm. Don't we have any thirtysomethings to hang out with instead? Are we so desperate to recapture our youth?"

Carmen's brows furrowed, and Lucy knew she'd pushed a well-buried button. Her friend often talked about how having a serious boyfriend so young had caused her to "miss out." Besides, if her family ever found out that she was gallivanting around with someone as young as Eddie, most of them would freak. A younger guy would be seen as a boy toy, and they were all ready for Carmen to finally tie the knot with the gold-stamped Malcolm.

But then the rebel got a hold of Carmen, as it always did. "Eddie's twenty-three. A graduate student in political science at UCSD. Age is just a number anyway."

"You keep telling yourself that," Lucy said, shaking her head. "Once we're checked into our MGM room, your hormones will have taken it down a notch and you'll be glad we escaped a bummer night."

Lucy made to start the car, but Carmen stopped her by placing a hand on the steering wheel. "Okay, yes, I'm amping out a little because he's so young, but what's one night?"

An eyebrow cock from Lucy was sufficient answer to

that. Looked like the breakup had changed all Carmen's big talk to action.

Her friend continued. "He seems like a safe kind of guy—and you must admit that I have good people radar—and it's not like anyone is ever going to know anyway. That's the beauty of the road...of strangers. We can drive away tomorrow morning and it won't matter."

A stranger...

A shock zinged through Lucy as she thought of the cowboy leaning against the wall, so near that she could smell the hint of grass on a breeze, of grit and smoke. Her breathing came harder as she fought the naughty craving of his fantasy. Of the improbable.

A tremble overtook her hands, but she overcame it by ignoring it. As usual.

Point A to point B...

There. Trembles...gone.

"Here's the thing," Carmen said, keeping her grip on the steering wheel, "and don't think any less of me for this. But consider the appeal. A stranger gets what he first sees, and there's very little judgment involved beyond an initial attraction. One night of fun will do wonders for the spirit, know what I mean? You could be as bad as you want to be and, as long as we're careful, there'd be no consequences unless we wanted to deal with them." Carmen wiggled her eyebrows. "How's that for some breakup-blues erasure?"

A pulse strummed in Lucy's neck. Pale eyes, devouring her from across the diner. Muscles beneath tanned skin and a worn T-shirt. A carnal appetite that gnawed at the lining of her belly.

She turned the ignition key, and Carmen's hand fell away from the steering wheel.

"First," Lucy said, "I could never think anything but good about you. Ever since college, we've spilled our guts to each other, no matter how goofy or embarrassing our secrets were."

"So we're off to the Timberline Inn?"

"Carm, I don't—"

A trilling ring from Carmen's canvas tote interrupted Lucy. When her friend checked the phone's screen, she cut off the call, then shut the device altogether, stuffing it back into her bag.

"Let me guess who that was," Lucy said over the sound of the idling engine.

"Malcolm, himself." Carmen ran a hand through her crazy hair. "It's bad enough that he ignores the fact that I broke up with him three weeks ago, but he showed up for dinner last night with the family."

"What?"

"I didn't say anything because I didn't want to put a damper on the festivities. I wanted to leave him behind."

"Is it like he's stalking you?"

"I'm pretty sure it's not stalking when Mama and my sisters all invite him over because they still think he's the one. They don't seem to understand that I *broke up* with him, and they're trying to persuade me to take him back."

"Then you should tell them about his extracurricular activities."

"I'm not ready."

Silence fell, and Lucy knew that Carmen had ended the discussion for now. Hitting the road would allow her friend to do more than just figure out a way to tell the brood that their beloved Malcolm was trash.

It would open a release valve for all the frustration her ex had put her through.

Lucy eased down the top on the car, then put the engine into gear so she could back out of the parking space. Afterward, when they'd reached the road, she turned the music off altogether, wanting to hear the tune of travel instead.

Wind blowing, tires humming over asphalt.

They passed a sign informing them that Calico Ghost Town, the first official noneating stop on the itinerary, was four miles away. Lucy headed toward the destination, realizing that she wasn't very excited about getting there, after all.

Something was dancing in the back of her mind, finally coming out of the dark: the cowboy, staying at the Timberline tonight.

Her cells crashed into each other, spinning alive.

Rationalization—or maybe it was Lucy's way of emerging—kicked in. Why was she forcing a friend who was also in need of some cheering up to go to a designated spot on an itinerary? Just because Lucy had planned it that way?

All the doubts of the day caught up with her as she came to the crossroads of Interstate 15 and the side road leading to their first scheduled stop.

Cowboys. Deviations.

An unplanned turn.

She'd done pretty well with taking a risk back at the diner with that cowboy, and she was going to be *thirty,* damn it.

So what the hell?

With a rush of screw-it rebellion, Lucy took the entrance to the road that would lead them to I-40.

And the Timberline Inn.

CARMEN'S WHOOP of approval had carried on the hair-blowing wind as the car picked up speed on the open road. She smiled, sticking her hand out of the window to surf the breezy waves that sped by.

But the best part? Lucy was smiling, too, as if she'd accomplished a big feat by shucking the itinerary.

That's my girl, Carmen thought. The breakup brigade was going to have some fly-by-the-pants fun, not that Carmen intended to get them into any trouble at this Timberline detour though. No way. Throughout college and beyond, she'd always kept an eye on Luce, just as her friend had watched out for her in return. Best friends till the end.

After flying through a stretch of desert filled with sienna-carved mountains and brown Historic Route 66 markers that indicated turnoffs for remnants of the Mother Road, they came to the junction of the 15 and 40.

"I'm guessing," Carmen yelled over the wind as they took the unexpected fork, "that we'll do Vegas another time? And we'll catch what we already missed of Route 66 on the way back?"

Lucy shrugged, suddenly all airy. Oh, Carmen liked this new attitude. Vacation was already taking them in exciting directions.

"We'll do what we can," her buddy yelled back, her loose, dark hair fluttering as they sped toward an adventure Carmen was practically hyperventilating about starting.

She leaned her head back on the rest, realizing that she was grinning like a *tonta.* A fool, for a guy named Eddie Kilpatrick, with young Leo DiCaprio–type hair and green eyes that held all sorts of enticing promises. Carmen didn't normally go for guys out of her age range. She hadn't ever even had a one-night stand, seeing as she'd been devoted to Malcolm for years…until she'd discovered that he'd been playing her so quietly and expertly.

What would it be like to have a fling?

Awesome, that was her answer, and she couldn't wait to see if it worked out.

Still...the good girl in her demanded to be heard. How would Mama and her sisters react if they ever found out? Not that they would, because Lucy always kept their secrets, but...

What were they going to do when Carmen told them about Malcolm's betrayal? Dad, with his honed father-suspicion, had accepted her old boyfriend only because Carmen had brought him home so long ago, and her judgment was good enough recommendation for him to play along until the breakup.

But Mama? *Ay,* Mama already had the wedding cake picked out and had been slyly leaving bridal magazines at Carmen's dinner-table spot for a while now.

Ah, forget it. Eddie was waiting, and Malcolm with his desperate kissing up to the Ferris women could go to...well, wherever bad boyfriends like him went.

It wasn't hard to find the Timberline Inn, which was just off the 40, next to a sparse selection of generic motels. The place had a reaching Yosemite air about it, with faux-log walls and spindly trees taking over for pines near the mostly empty parking lot.

Inside their room, the TV was small, yet serviceable, and the furnishings were clean, if not comfortably worn. Luckily, the quilted patterns of the bedspreads covered a lot of traffic, as Carmen found loose threads among the gingham and paisley squares.

"Five star," Lucy said, hands on her slim hips as she surveyed the bed.

"You wanted the ruggedness of Route 66, and you got it. And we're not even officially on that stretch yet."

Lucy heaved her suitcase onto the mattress. "You're right. Cheap hotels and even cheaper comfort food. An adventure."

"To our grand adventure."

Carmen pretended to toast Lucy, who responded with a modest glee that warmed the heart. Two pals blazing trails together. Who knew what tonight might have in store for each of them?

"What do you say we go to the pool," Carmen said, digging through her luggage for her bikini, "then grab a bite at the coffee shop. After, we'll get ready for the festivities."

Lucy nodded, then paused, a giddy grin on her lips. "Carm?"

"Yeah?"

The grin grew. "We're on *vacation*."

Carmen knew exactly what her friend meant. Freedom away from their jobs, their real lives. Liberty from the expectation that defined them.

Yes!

But first, Lucy called the MGM to cancel the room and then phoned her older brother, Jonathan, mentioning where they were and what they intended to do tonight. Jonathan, whom Lucy treated like one of her best friends, laughed and told them to watch themselves. And they would.

Then they dorked around the well-kempt pool, soaking in the spring sun and reading books—a Queen Elizabeth I biography for Carmen and a werewolf novel for Lucy—because the water hadn't been sufficiently heated. Then, after downing salads in the dark-paneled coffee shop, they showered and got ready for their evening.

At one point, Lucy asked what they would do if Eddie and

friends ended up ditching them, but Carmen knew he would be calling her cell phone once he checked in. He'd promised, and she recognized the look in a man's gaze when he meant it.

Just as she'd recognized Malcolm's lies when he'd started to avoid eye contact.

Maybe that's what had drawn her to Eddie, as unsuitable as he was for her: his openness, his energy and charm. And was he ever charming. Just talking to him had warmed Carmen up inside. Since things had gone downhill with Malcolm—even before she'd caught him sharing his attentions with other women—she'd missed feeling such an instant attraction, such pure awareness of a male.

But at 7:00 p.m., when her phone hadn't rung yet, she started to get worried…until Lucy pointed out that Carmen had shut off the device earlier.

D-oh. Upon turning the phone on, there it was. A message from Eddie.

"Hope you came," he said, and she couldn't help dwelling on the "came" part as he mentioned his room number and a good time to stop by.

If her bite was as real as her bark, she just *might* come tonight. She just might celebrate being away from all the pressures Malcolm and her family had saddled her with lately.

Adrenaline shot through her, and she wasn't sure if it was because she was giddy or even a little fearful of straying from her old comfort zone…

Carmen fixed a looped earring to her lobe and wandered to where Lucy was brushing on mascara by the mirror. "T-minus five minutes and counting."

She stopped in her tracks at the sight of her friend, who was wearing a wispy beige sheath decorated with maroon flowers and lace. The hues brought out Lucy's fresh coloring to a startling degree.

Generally, Lucy had no idea how gorgeous she was. She *never* had and, in effect, she tended to push her boyfriends into speeding up their relationship, as if she were racing to an engagement before the guy found out he didn't want to be with her. That had no doubt come from the snowball effect of Lucy's first high-school breakup, then the next, each escalating her doubts about being attractive or valuable.

Lucy turned to inspect Carmen, who was decked out in her own party ensemble: go-go boots coupled with a short white skirt and halter. She'd fluffed out her short red hair, too, so it came off a bit witchy and cool.

"The fabled hot-stuff boots," Lucy said. "Poor Eddie doesn't have a chance."

"Just what I'm hoping."

Carmen linked arms with her pal, and they left the room, heading for number 176.

The pounding bass from an old AC/DC song led them to an empty section of the motel. Not as if it was all that busy anyway, but it was good to see from the echoing parking lot that they wouldn't be bugging people with noise.

The door was open, and they wandered in to find two members of Eddie's group dancing on a bed to a boom box, beer bottles held aloft. One was a ginger-headed boy candidate for the Nickelodeon Channel and the other was the curly-headed blond girl who'd squealed "par-tay!" at the diner earlier.

The rest of the group sat at a table, bouncing quarters off its surface.

Carmen's heart sank. Where was…?

A Lindsay Lohan look-alike who was playing Quarters

waved to them, causing everyone else to notice that they'd entered.

"Hey! Eddie's getting some ice!" she said.

As if summoned, a voice smoothed over Carmen's back, just like fingers trailing up her skin.

"Welcome to our humble establishment," Eddie said.

Buzzing, Carmen lost track of Lucy's reaction, although she knew that her friend must've turned around to see him at the same time.

All she truly realized was that something had gone tight inside her, low and hot, beating and wet with a desire she recognized as the hope she'd felt back when she believed in everlasting, exciting love.

Just one night with Eddie and everything he makes me remember about being younger and less brokenhearted, she thought. *And no one will ever know.*

ONCE EDDIE HAD COME on the scene to enchant Carmen, Lucy knew it was time to make some new friends.

It wasn't long before she found herself sitting at the table with the four other partiers while Carmen and Eddie created their own private, invisible space bubble.

They stood near the vanity area right now, Eddie towering over Carmen as they laughed with each other, touched each other on the arm, on the shoulder. And when Carmen reacted to what must've been a particularly funny comment, she leaned back her head and placed a hand on his chest.

The master, Lucy thought, wondering if she could ever be just as adept at flirting.

Images of the cowboy flooded her, washing through her body until she stirred in her seat with achy discomfort.

"Let's do this, Lucky!" one of the boys at her table yelled, handing her the quarter she was supposed to ping off the table to land in a plastic beer cup.

They'd taken to calling her a nickname already, and with a few sips of alchie in her, she didn't mind.

Taking aim, she nonetheless missed the cup with the quarter and had to drink from her own bottle.

"Lu-cky, Lu-cky," they chanted as she withstood her punishment.

When she finished, she daintily slammed her bottle to the surface, and they liked that, cheering her.

Not that she even had a buzz on. Oh, heck no. Lucy had inherited a tolerance for booze from her parents, who liked their nightly martinis after work. It was a cute routine, very fifties like. In fact, Mom and Pop Christie reminded Lucy a lot of a throwback couple. She and Jonathan had kidded on more than one occasion about how their parents must've had sex only two times and then slept in separate beds like on the *Dick Van Dyke Show.*

Nonetheless, Lucy wished she could find the security of always having someone around who loved her. Her parents had it—she should, too.

Out of the corner of her eye, she saw Eddie lean down to whisper something in Carmen's ear. When he came up, they stared at each other, smiling.

Lucy picked at the label on her beer bottle. She wanted her cowboy, just as Carmen had her own adventure for the night.

Had *he* checked in yet? Was there a chance he might hear the music coming from this room and wander in?

Maybe the college guy next to Lucy picked up on that steamy vibe, because he leaned in close to her, pressing arm against arm. He was wearing too much cologne, like most young males did in some kind of misunderstood mating ritual.

"You need another drink?" he asked.

She shook her head, thinking he reminded her of Roy Rogers. An affable smile. Sparkling, squinty eyes.

But he was no cowboy, she thought, recalling a much more dangerous variation: one who hadn't really smiled today at the diner.

One who had lingered in the shadows where he seemed terribly comfortable.

The music got louder to her, even though no one had turned it up. But it was Led Zeppelin, so she didn't really mind. What she *did* mind, however, was Roy Rogers's hand creeping onto her thigh.

She stood, backing away from the table. God, what was she doing here with these kids? All of them looked so, so *young*, and she didn't belong. Not at this party, not on this trip.

How could she have thought otherwise?

"Go on without me," she said as the crowd protested her leaving.

"Aw," another guy said. Earlier, he'd told her he was from the Philippines. "Come on, Lucky! We need more girls for Seven Minutes in Heaven!"

Was he talking about the game where two people went into a closet or bathroom and locked the door for seven minutes with the lights out? He had to be joking.

But when Lucy approached Carmen, she saw that her friend, who was drinking from a bottle of soda, was taking the suggestion quite enthusiastically. She and Eddie grinned at each other as he jerked his head toward the bathroom.

Carmen laughed just as Lucy approached.

"I'm going to hit the sack," Lucy said.

"Already?" Carmen asked.

"I think I've already overstayed." She leaned over to her friend to whisper, "I won't expect you back tonight?"

Carmen shrugged, looking mischievous and hopeful.

"Okay." Lucy made a smug face, happy that a post-breakup Carmen was having a good time. Mal could eat it. "Then I'm off."

"Wait, let me walk you to the room."

Oh, right, like Lucy was going to shatter the clear sexual tension between her friend and the boy toy. Not a chance. Before Carmen had committed to Malcolm in college, she'd always had a wild streak ten miles wide, but she'd never gone all the way with it—just lots of innocuous flirting, really. Yet after she'd settled down with Malcolm, a sedate Carmen had quietly wondered what it would be like to test that streak and, now that she was free, she had all the room in the world to do it.

Frankly, Carmen deserved a prize for what Mal had done to her.

"No, stay here," Lucy said. "We're just in the next building, and the coffee shop, then the office, are a few doors down from our room. Besides, this place is hardly threatening."

"Lucy..."

"I forbid it, Carm." She added a wink, but Carmen still seemed doubtful.

So Lucy turned to Eddie. "Keep her here, okay? I'll call when I get to my room if it makes a difference."

"It does," Carmen said.

Eddie grinned, and Lucy could see why Carmen was so taken. "Maybe this is a sign that you should just stay," he said.

"No, really." Lucy performed a yawn, and carried it off pretty well, actually. "Lots of driving tomorrow."

With a mock punch to Carmen's arm and a be-careful-you-scamp glance, Lucy made for the door.

"Call in two minutes?" Carmen asked over the music.

Lucy took out her cell from her purse, raised her hand to show Carmen that she was ready to phone for help if needed. Then she concentrated on resisting more drunken pleas to stay from the Quarters table. Of course, she buh-byed them, then finished her beer and tossed the bottle into a wastebasket.

Once outside, she meandered toward her room, breathing in the early night's air. The party music settled to a punching kick as she got farther away.

And each kick felt like a new pulse of loneliness.

She wished she was as spirited as Carmen, wished she felt so good about herself that attracting another man would be effortless.

She passed the office, the coffee shop. Then, just yards away from her room, something caught her attention.

It was a stirring in the wind. As if the restaurant's door had opened and shut.

But when she turned around, nothing was there except shadows.

Shadows like the ones that had hidden the cowboy at the diner today.

Adrenaline was streaming through her now, and she got out the tarnished key, pushing it into the lock, opening her door. Then she dialed Carmen, who answered immediately.

"You inside?"

A mere technicality, since Lucy was in the process of shutting the door. "Yes, party animal. Have a good time."

"You, too, sleepyhead. See you soon."

They disconnected. And…there it was again.

That slight variation in the air.

Heart in her throat, Lucy's eyes focused through the slit in her door to find *him* yards away, half swallowed by shade and night.

The cowboy, leaning against the wall with his hands in his pockets, slim-hipped yet roped with sinew and muscle. His silvered eyes cut through the darkness, aided by a slash of light.

But instead of being afraid, Lucy's pulse started to go a little wild.

3

JOSHUA HAD NO DAMN idea what he was doing outside the brunette's room.

But what was new? He hadn't possessed an inkling of what was going on inside his own head back at Peggy Sue's 50's Diner, either, when she had left him on sexual tenterhooks with her mysterious smile.

The image of her had lingered all day, even after he'd arrived at the Timberline, where he'd taken dinner at the coffee shop, paid up, then brooded over coffee.

Thinking of her, wanting her.

Then, as if he had conjured her right out of his dreams, she'd strolled by the restaurant's window, her hair in those breezy waves, her lithe figure garbed in a light dress that reminded him of petals under a gold moon. His belly had clutched so hard that he had thought he might collapse into himself from pure agony.

Damn, all it took to get him going was the mere sight of her. What did this make him? A desperate man?

Good God, once she saw him, what would she think about him following her from the restaurant and coming to stand near her room?

Hi, he could say. *Fancy accidentally running into* you *here at the Timberline Inn, where I thought there might be a small chance you'd show up tonight, even though you told me you wouldn't.*

But then, without another thought, he'd risen from his seat, intent on…

Doing what? Saying hello? Frightening her half to death by sneaking up behind her while she unlocked her room?

He'd come within yards of her, hesitating. His basic decency told him to leave the brunette be.

But his body? It had screamed a different argument, one much more immediate and persuasive.

As she had unlocked her door and made a short phone call, he'd leaned against the log wall, not wishing to seem a threat, even though he knew he might come off that way. And he wouldn't blame her if she thought so, either. Maybe he just wasn't good for anyone: not this brunette, not his neighbor back home…not even himself.

Then it happened.

She saw him standing there, and she froze, protected by her door as she peered around it, waiting in tense silence to see what he might do next.

"Hope I didn't scare you any," he said softly, wishing he had just followed his common sense and gone to his own room. Nothing positive could come of this mood he'd been in ever since he'd left Fielding.

Even so, at the same time, he wished she would open that door a little wider to him.

She kept peering through the door's crack. Then something seemed to switch on inside her, although he couldn't be sure with just the moonlight as a guide.

The door opened an inch wider.

"I was just in the restaurant," he said, calming his goaded

desire. "They serve a hell of a rib-eye steak here. But then you showed up, contrary to my advice."

Even yards away, she was too close for him to resist, and it was beyond him to do any backing off anyway. Not here, not now, when the sight of her was so unnerving, setting his flesh to crackling. Charging him up just because of the way she was looking at him.

He slid his hat off and held it to his chest, standing away from the wall and taking a step closer.

"Did things go well at your party?" he asked.

Had she parted her door even wider at his cautious approach? No, he had to be imagining it.

"It was all right," she said. "Totally predictable though."

"And that's not what you wanted?"

He cut himself off before he said too much. If she knew what *he* wanted, she'd slam that door in his face, leaving him anguished and starved. It'd be another failure to notch into his tarnished lighter case, another reason to feel irrelevant in a world that tended to spit a person out when they weren't worthy enough.

God, he needed a win to bolster him after having lost so badly in Fielding. He needed to matter this one time, because maybe it would get him back into sane, working order.

So he took another step. Then another.

Now he could hear her breathing: short, choppy. Excited?

Her reaction weaved through him, tightening his body until it began to throb.

One more step.

He was two feet from the door now, and she still hadn't shut him out. In fact, her eyes had widened even more, and he took that as an opening.

"I've been cautious all night about your warnings," she said, "so maybe I wasn't up for all that mingling with people I barely knew."

"And now?"

He smiled—it was easier this time. Besides, he had to let her know that he wasn't anyone to be afraid of. That he could be deserving of just one night where he could talk to her and maybe begin to feel normal again.

"Now?" she asked. "*You're* still a stranger only a few feet outside my motel door."

"I can introduce myself properly. Show you my driver's license so you'd know my name and address."

"And what if I don't want to know your name?"

Sassy. She was in control here, wasn't she? And he'd thought she might be shy. Hell, not this woman.

But how did she manage to stay so sweet in spite of it all? How did she enthrall him, spreading bursts of yearning like shotgun blasts until they settled in his cock with a painful, building pressure?

"You don't have to know my name," he said, "to come back to the coffee shop with me."

Because that was a good start, right? Talking with a woman who didn't know he'd been beaten and hung out to dry by a neighbor he'd trusted back home. This brunette looked at him as if he had the potential to save a ranch that had been handed down through the family generation after generation, and that mattered to Joshua.

Mattered a lot.

Besides, who knew what might happen after a talk in a coffee shop?

"Do they know your name at the restaurant here?" she

asked, opening the door wide enough to lean her head against it.

A strand in his chest wrapped around its dark self, twining into a rope that creaked with the tension of being pulled and twisted.

"The waitress and cashier saw my name on my credit card and acted like we were on a first-name basis at the end there," he said. "And the desk clerk took down all but my last blood pressure reading when I checked into my room. I guess that means they know me as much as I care to introduce myself."

Something he said must've gotten to her. Because, at that moment, she changed expression, smiling with a confidence that took the oxygen straight out of his lungs.

Then she opened her door all the way to him.

MAYBE LUCY WAS CRAZY, but the fact that the motel had the cowboy's personal information goaded her into taking the next step into a true vacation.

A fantasy. A flirtation with a stranger.

A true game changer in a life that sorely needed to be shaken up.

Would she regret what she was about to do? Or would she, indeed, be able to drive off into the new horizon as a liberated woman?

But then she took a stand with herself. She'd spent thirty years living carefully, and now it was time to try a place less traveled.

Throat dry, she swallowed, then went for it, just as she had earlier in the day when she'd changed direction and thrown her plans to the wind.

"Want to…?" She gestured inside the room, inviting him in.

He paused, as if surprised, and, for a second, Lucy thought

he might refuse her. How mortifying. How expected, too, because women like her didn't carry through with fantasies like this. Something always thwarted the reality of them.

But then he moved forward. Once over the threshold, he became a muscled silhouette in the moonlit darkness, and she breathed him in, becoming dizzy with the scent of pungent grass and spirits—the thought of true freedom.

Just do it, Lucy, she thought, heart pummeling her chest. *For the first time in your life, just do what you want and then let it go.*

His shadow reached for the light switch in the dim room, but she stopped him.

"Don't."

When he paused, she realized that maybe he hadn't been expecting her to be so forward, even if she had invited him into her room.

A kiss in the dark, she thought. No names, no faces, just a dream that wouldn't seem quite real.

No one would ever know.

The realization made her feel more powerful than she'd ever thought possible, and it felt…right.

Swept up by the buzz of her bravery, she pushed her inhibitions away, taking hold of his cowboy hat and tossing it aside.

He laughed at that, the timbre low, half surprised, half amused.

She laughed a little, herself. This was her—the woman who had been hiding in a closet stocked with stark uniforms. But she was coming out full force now, grasping his T-shirt, pulling him toward her for the kiss she'd been craving since this afternoon.

Go, Lucy, go…

The contact was startling, a break in the straight line of her world. A flare of searing light blinded her and then began to pulsate with the thick tempo of her blood.

He tasted like coffee, hard alcohol, male. His stubble did burn, just as she'd fantasized, but his lips were full and soft as he responded to her overture with a ragged groan.

Slipping his hands into her hair, he held her as if he didn't want her to escape, as if he'd been half hoping this would happen but couldn't believe it'd come to fruition. And when he slid his tongue into her mouth, taking the kiss to a more sensual level, the ache she'd felt earlier while merely watching him across the diner returned, banging, clenching, piercing her with a stretched longing to be satisfied.

Satisfied. What would that finally be like?

She could feel herself getting wet already, even with only a kiss. A rough, tumbled, moist play of lips and tongue. A ravishment that sent all her blood from her head to the sensitive area growing so plump between her legs.

Coming up for breath, she rubbed her cheek against his, loving the scratch of his skin. She tugged at his longish, dark hair with one hand, running the other over his firm chest.

Who are you? she wanted to ask, even though she told herself that she didn't want to know. Not if she wished to cut loose tomorrow. Not if she wanted to prove that she didn't have to be the one who was always left behind.

His mouth devoured hers as he guided her backward, toward the wall. Something like panic—no, it was unadulterated joy—seized her.

It's actually happening... A wicked time with a man who won't be around long enough to leave you.

They stumbled, bodies plastered together, unwilling to separate even for a moment.

As they bolted against the wall, the cowboy cushioned the impact with his arms, cradling her. Then, panting against her mouth, he deliberately smoothed his hands downward, mapping every plane: her shoulder blades, her waist, her hipbones.

Then he came to her ass, and he pushed her forward as he cupped her, kneading her cheeks.

Lucy swallowed a gasp. His long fingers were so close to her swollen folds that each massage was pure agony. And now…now… Oh.

He was pressing her against an impressive erection. Unable to help herself, she wiggled against him, wanting as much as she could get.

This was going to be more than just a kiss or a few copped feels. Hell, yeah, it was.

Grunting, he coasted his hands lower, until he palmed the back of her thighs. His fingers stayed busy, stroking her sensitized skin.

"Are you sure…?" he asked, dipping down to kiss her neck.

Was he asking if she was regretting this? Hardly.

"Just keep on doing what you're doing," she said, short of breath. Short of patience.

He rose up slightly to look at her face, but she doubted he could see much with the only light coming from a slit of moon glow between the heavy curtains.

But, still, she could imagine him searching her eyes for a clue as to what she was all about.

She wished she knew the definitive answer, too.

Then he did something she didn't expect: he kissed her again, a gentle touch of his mouth to hers. No rough insistence. No animal passion.

The switch of pace jarred her and, for the first time, she

did feel threatened. This wasn't what she wanted from a one-night-stand fantasy. It was *too* intimate, which was ironic considering what had happened so far.

Out of a sense of personal preservation, Lucy instinctively reached down to feel his crotch. Rigid, big… She wanted him inside her, that's all. Wanted to know what it would be like to enjoy pure physical pleasure with no momentous expectations attached.

She rubbed him, and he hitched in a breath, tightening his hold on her thighs.

"Wait," she whispered, feeling more empowered by the second. "I just want it…naughty. Can you give me that?"

When she lightly squeezed his penis, he made a strangled noise low in his throat.

Then, before she knew what was happening, she got her wish.

As if wanting to regain some kind of control, too, he whipped her around until her front was flush against the smooth wall. Just as efficiently, he took her hands and raised them, resting his own arms against hers, his chest against her back. She felt him fighting for oxygen, felt his arousal insinuating itself between her legs.

Stimulated, she rocked back against him, and he threaded his fingers through hers. The texture of his rough palms over her softer skin was shocking, digging into a primitive part of her that banged out a jungle rhythm.

"I didn't think you'd be up for naughty," he said against her ear. His words were hot, moist. "Not even when you opened your door to me."

I didn't think so, either, she thought.

"What did you expect?" she managed to gasp, cheek against the wall.

Slowly, he slid his hands down her arms. Her dress stuck to her with emerging sweat, and his own perspiration mixed with the air, carnal, overcoming her, braiding into her.

"From you?" he whispered. "I expected lemonade on a humid day."

He eased his hands to the front of her body, where his fingers taunted her breasts. Lucy's legs gelled, but he held her up by inserting a thigh between her legs. She tingled there, her clit assuaged by the contact.

"I expected," he continued, squeezing her breasts, "root-beer candy from a sweets store's barrel."

She couldn't stand this: the teasing words, the building pressure thudding to get out.

"And what did you get?" she couldn't help asking, hoping he saw the new Lucy and not the old, drab one.

I'm really doing this…

He paused, as if in thought, then with a more forceful touch, he coaxed his hands down her ribs, her belly. Her muscles jumped, shuddering and breaking her down bit by bit.

"I'm not certain what I'm getting," he rasped, "but I'm intent on finding out."

With that, he got down to his knees, reaching under her dress at the same moment to drag her undies with him. At the whisper of air between her legs, Lucy shivered, exposed.

And it was about time.

As she stepped out of her underwear, she wondered what he was going to do. She suspected…wished…

From below, he guided her to spread her legs for him, and she shakily obliged, leaning her arms fully against the wall because she knew she would wither any second.

Slowly—damn it, so slowly—the cowboy traced his fingers up the inside of her calves, over the backs of her knees.

Lucy flinched. She even winced, every cell pulsating in straining greed.

When is he going to…?

Frantic and trembling, she braced herself while he traveled his palms up the backs of her thighs and under her dress, giving him a view of her bare ass.

He kept her skirt raised with one hand while caressing a cheek with his other.

"Look what these long legs lead to," he whispered, his tone battered.

She'd never thought of her legs as long, just…gangly. And she'd never known that a man could comment so reverently about any part of her body.

"You can't even see anything in this room," she said into her arm, which had come to cradle her head while she held herself up.

Quaking now. Jeez, she was shivering so badly that she thought she might burst into a shower of static.

"Maybe I can't see all that well," he said, "but I can sure as hell feel."

He traced his fingers under the crease of her cheek, then pushed up, as if he couldn't get enough of her curves.

Just when she thought she couldn't take any more, he urged her to spread her legs wider, and he kissed the backs of her knees, then delved under her dress to worship the inside of her thighs. He licked her, no doubt tasting the juices that were now coating her skin.

It felt as if she were being wedged open from her core outward. Split apart, torn and anguished. But in a good way.

Such a good way.

As his fingers parted her cheeks, her folds, Lucy stiffened, knowing what was coming now.

Please, have it be coming now...

His tongue made contact with her, and she cried out, slumping against the wall.

But his strong hands kept her up as he deepened this particular kiss, his tongue laving her, seeking out her clit and circling it.

Can't believe this is happening...

Just as she was on the edge of scratching at the wall with pent-up, drenched tension, he adjusted position, maneuvering himself faceup and bringing her down until she was on her knees, over his mouth as he lay back on the floor.

By this time, her eyes had adjusted to the dimness of the room, and she watched the vague sight of him clutching her hips, then guiding her the rest of the way down to kiss her between the legs again. Spellbound, Lucy lifted her dress, wanting to see him loving her, even if it mostly meant conjuring the rest of the images in her mind's eye.

He pulled at her, sipping and taking his leisurely time, and she braced one hand against the wall, keeping her balance as she started tearing in half again. She churned with the cadence of his tongue, the sucking of her lips into his mouth.

As she reared back her head, she lost herself in the seething crevice that her torn body created. Her mind went dark, numb and blank as she felt herself falling backward, not knowing what she was diving into as she spread her arms and parted her lips in an ecstatic smile she'd never believed herself capable of...

Then, without warning, she blew apart, flying up, high, so high as she emerged from that crevice...

A higher consciousness, a new birth.

A new Lucy.

As she rode the pain, the air, she groaned. It could've been for a minute. Maybe an hour…

All she knew was that, at some point, he picked her up, his breath coming harsh and quick. She pressed against him, wrapping her legs around his waist as he fumbled with his wallet, then a package, then his fly.

He knocked a lamp off a table, and she found herself sitting on the glossy surface, desperate for breath and for him, knowing that if he didn't come inside her soon she was going to explode again.

She helped him sheathe himself, then guided him to her beating sex—drenched and ready.

He thrust into her, and she heaved in an excited gasp at his size, at his arousal filling her so thoroughly. Pumping, straining, he kept going deeper, and she arched against him, reaching one arm back to grab the edge of the table so she could take him harder, longer.

He answered her churn for churn. Each jab dug into her deeper, pulling her out of body, inch…by inch…by…

When she climaxed for the second time, it was as if she'd been let out of a cage, free to fly toward the sun until the tips of her wings were scorched.

Then she fell once again, free, rushing toward the ground—

As she tumbled off the table, the cowboy caught her, easing her the rest of the way to the floor, where he strained, then spilled his come with a final push.

Then he collapsed at her side, and Lucy's first instinct was to hold him close, to keep him inside her.

But she knew better this time.

Part of the fantasy was to let go.

JOSHUA HAD FALLEN to pieces at his shattering climax. Then wonderfully, *miraculously,* as he began putting himself back together again, he finally found the man he had been looking for.

The man he had lost back home.

He grasped for a regular semblance of breathing, of existing. Yet the second his partner slid off his cock, he felt everything disappear.

He wanted to reach for her, to grab her and hold on to the sweat-soaked serenity of the moment. He wanted to keep it all—the power, the electricity, the connection that had just brought him back to life.

But she had already moved away from him, smoothing down her dress in the dim light allowed by the curtains.

When his adjusted sight focused enough for him to see that she had even gone a step farther, running her hands over the carpet while searching for her panties, his chest tightened.

What had he expected? He'd all but asked for easy, quick sex, and he had gotten it. In spades.

So why did it feel so hollow now that it was over?

Why hadn't the healing lasted?

Joshua knew what he needed: more. He wanted to bang her again, to get back that fleeting feeling of being all man, all dominant male again.

"Leaving already?" he asked.

"I can't leave. This is my room, remember?"

He could barely see her easing the panties up her legs. Those long, beautiful legs.

Just thinking of her body, her soft skin, her wet vaginal passage, made him stir. And this reminded him that he was still wearing the condom, so he rose to dispose of it.

When he came back, his fly zipped but his emotions hardly as restrained, she was standing near the door, having flicked on the light switch. A broken lamp littered the floor, and he recalled having knocked it over in the heat of the moment.

It shed dim, off-kilter illumination, breeding shadows from the ground up. The effect was unsettling, especially when it was coupled with the cool sheen of the brunette's demeanor.

She didn't seem unfriendly at all. No, just…done. It took a moment for Joshua to realize that.

His hunger—sorely fed and hardly assuaged—bit at him. He couldn't believe there wouldn't be more, couldn't believe their encounter had obviously meant so little to her when it had been such an answer for him.

He tried to shake off the ridiculous sentiments. Tried hard, because all it had been was a one-night stand. An easy fix for a problem much more significant.

Picking his wallet up off the floor, he extracted enough to cover the cost of the lamp. "I'll take care of the damage."

"No, don't worry about it. I've got it covered."

She laughed, almost as if she couldn't believe what had transpired and was just now acknowledging it. He realized that her earlier cool sheen might have been, in truth, an after-glow—a happy flush that sex had brought to the surface.

But he wasn't sure. Not with the way she was keeping her distance from him.

"I wonder," he said, attempting to lift the heavy awkwardness, "how many lamps a motel has to go through during any given week."

"I couldn't even start to guess."

She caught his eye, then glanced away, her flush blooming like a stain. Embarrassed? he wondered. Maybe he'd been right about her not being the type to have this kind of quickie.

So what had just happened?

"Listen..." he started.

But that seemed to be her cue to end any more attempts at levity. Tonight was what it was, no sense in pretending otherwise.

She wandered toward the door, smoothing her hair back over an ear.

As sure a sign as any. She'd gotten what she wanted and now it was time for him to leave. Joshua certainly didn't believe in pushing a moment when a woman was being so clear, but, then again, that didn't mean he wanted to go.

More. He wanted *more.*

Still, while she wasn't looking, he sneaked the wad of bills under the crease of pillow on the bed nearest him, hoping it wouldn't come off like he was paying her or something. He wanted to be responsible for that lamp—that was all. Then he made his way to the exit.

When he got there, he hesitated, risking enough to stand only inches away from her. He couldn't stop himself.

"What's your name?" he asked softly, maybe because he needed closure. Maybe because he couldn't let go this time.

For a moment, he thought he had her. Her eyes went as blue as a pool where two people might embrace, their bare skin slick and sliding while they came together. Her berry-stained lips parted, just as they had back in the gift shop, when he'd first seen that she wanted him.

When he'd decided to pursue her.

Yet then, something came over her, a second thought. A reconsideration.

And any chance of getting more ended right there.

"No names," she repeated from earlier, clearly meaning it. "Not for us strangers."

Knowing that she was right, Joshua nodded, then left the room with her standing at the door, then closing it behind him.

Yup, she was right about keeping their names out of it. So he'd just stop thinking about the woman with the deep blue eyes and mysterious smile. He'd stop thinking about what her friends might call her, too.

He just wished knowing her name didn't matter more than anything else at this moment.

4

BACK AT THE PARTY, Carmen had put her phone away, relieved that Lucy had called to say she was safe.

"All tucked in for the night," she said.

Eddie was still standing by her side at the sink. "You two keep an eye out for each other, don't you?"

"Ever since we were little freshmen studentlings. But... well, that was ages ago."

Suddenly all too aware of the years she had on him—good heavens, *seven*—she shook her head, took a drink and put her beverage on the counter. Had Lucy been right when she'd asked earlier if Carmen just wanted to recapture her youth by coming to his room?

Maybe Lucy was right. After spending most of college dating Malcolm only to lose all the time and emotion she'd invested in him, Carmen felt as if she truly *could've* missed something vital that all the other kids had gained. What it was, she had no idea, but here she was testing its waters now.

A vintage Aerosmith song took over the boom box, and Eddie clasped her hand, rubbing his thumb over hers. Then he leaned in close, talking in her ear so she could hear over the music. He stirred her hair, warmed her ear.

"You look a million miles away," he said.

Great, she was a real upper. Tonight was supposed to be

about fun, plain and simple: making up for all the time she'd lost.

"I'm just taking it all in," she said, raising her own voice to compete with the lyrics.

He gave her a long look, then a smile that made her blood purr.

At the Quarters table, everyone cheered, and one of the guys stood—the kid from the Philippines—and gulped down his beer. All the others banged their fists on the table, urging him on.

Eddie leaned over again. "Two days ago it was Richie's twenty-first birthday." He gestured toward the beer-swilling partier. "He was the last one to turn completely legal, and they're all still celebrating."

He said it as if he was somehow distanced from the rest of the group. Hmm, curiouser and curiouser.

Just as she was about to pursue the subject, he got a devilish gleam in his green eyes, then jerked his chin toward the bathroom.

Carmen gave him an arch look. Earlier, when the subject of Seven Minutes in Heaven had come up, they'd traded flirty expressions, joking and almost daring each other to take up the game.

Now, as he pulled her away from the sink area, her heart rate picked up speed.

"Where do you think you're taking me?" she asked lightly.

He didn't answer, just kept leading her toward the restroom.

"You've got to be kidding," she said, even though this was what she'd wanted. Right? This was what everything had been leading up to.

Scenarios flitted past her mind's eye, each one building in speed and urgency until she felt their culmination in the pump of her pulse. Him, tearing her halter top off… Him, latching his mouth to her breast… Her, grinding into him…

By the time he'd closed the door behind them, Carmen was already seduced. A shiver of white heat bolted over her skin, flashing it with dampness. An ache to be touched.

What would it be like to have a party fling, just as she probably should've done in college?

Then again, it wasn't as if she could replay the past and make sure it went right this time. She couldn't correct all the decisions she had made to be faithful to what she thought she had wanted back then.

But she was overthinking.

Easy, breezy sex, she mused. That's all this had to be.

"Seven minutes," she said, backing away from him until her calves hit the bathtub. "Is that really all we get in here?"

"Those are the rules."

Oh, and there it was again—that killer grin.

Behind the closed door, the party sounds were muted enough to make it feel as if they'd gone into some private little world of their own. And when he secured the lock, it drove the point home.

Carmen told herself to breathe, just breathe. Damn, shouldn't she be more confident as an older woman? Mrs. Robinson sure was. Not that Carmen was quite that mature, but…

Desire pounded to her head, and it felt as if she were processing everything in a vacuum. Maybe that's why he seemed to take five hours to move closer to her.

But when he finally arrived, he surprised her by pausing, stuffing his hands into his back pockets while he gauged her.

Good Lord, she didn't want him to see she was nervous. That'd be truly pathetic, a thirty-year-old one-night-stand virgin.

"You ever done your time in Heaven before?" she asked, trying to regain her equilibrium.

"Raised on the game." Eddie looked terribly serious in a playful sort of way.

"I remember reading *Are You There God? It's Me, Margaret* when I was young. Didn't she and her crush spend seven minutes in a closet in that book? I can't recall very well. Or maybe you didn't—" she gulped "—read it."

"No, I didn't, Carmen," he said.

Of course, it was a chick book. The basic bible for adolescent girls. Why had she even asked?

Because she was babbling. Her. Carmen Ferris, apparent wild child.

Her heart kept doing roundhouse kicks to her chest and it only got worse as Eddie stepped nearer.

Just a whisper away.

"How much time have we got left?" she asked, trying to tease. But she didn't sound very convincing. "Five minutes?"

"I haven't even started the clock."

He bent even closer, taking his hands out of his pockets and cupping her face. Long fingers, she thought, nice hands…

She took in a lungful of oxygen, bracing herself for her first encounter with a guy since Malcolm. Actually, as far as anything sexual went, her ex had been her first, her only…

Eddie had paused a sigh away from her lips.

That's when Carmen realized that she'd gone stiff, like a girl who was awaiting a first kiss and didn't know what to expect.

Wild child, indeed.

"You okay with this?" Eddie almost seemed amused.

She exhaled, but it did nothing to ease her furious heartbeat. "I'll be honest. I don't do much messing around."

They were still so close that she was forced to talk softly, almost brushing his lips with hers.

"Ah," he said, backing away, but only slightly. And he didn't remove his hands from her face, either. In fact, he explored her cheeks with his thumbs, strumming her.

Carmen closed her eyes, well played, vibrations seeping downward until they pooled in a spot that had been buzzing in limbo since they'd come in here.

"Sorry," she said, laughing a little to lighten the moment. "Here I am, the older woman, and I've only had a blip of dating experience."

"A blip."

"I mean that I dated the same guy for years when most everyone else was running around experimenting."

"The same guy, huh?"

One of his hands was now stroking her hair back, and she all but melted. She was a total sucker for hair play.

"I'm not with him now," she added. "We recently broke up. All that history, down the drain."

He listened, stroking, looking into her eyes. It was easy to keep going on.

So she did, finding herself spilling the beans about Malcolm and his cheating. Eddie kept listening—patient and in no hurry for her to finish.

"I even think," she continued, "that the worst part wasn't the breakup. That turned out to be a blessing, because ending things with Malcolm didn't even hurt that much. We'd gone different directions, started drifting apart. It was his lying that got to me. The feeling that I'd been such an idiot and hadn't seen any of it happening right beneath my nose."

Eddie nodded, his fingers traveling down to her neck, where he caressed the tender dip between her collarbones. She swayed at the sharp sensation, the pierce of need that split her.

Head fuzzy, her eyelids went heavy, and her next words barely made it out of her mouth.

"It's never going to happen again," she said. "Being left in the dark."

And maybe *that's* why she'd come to Eddie tonight: because, with a stranger, lies probably wouldn't be important.

She took in his scent: his skin, clean and fresh. It washed through her, a soothing rush.

"If you don't like the dark," Eddie whispered, "we'll just leave the light on."

She couldn't stand it anymore. The tension between them finally snapped and pulled her toward him.

As she pressed her lips against his, every fiber connecting her sizzled. She was wired with longing, stimulated by the softness of a kiss.

He folded her in his arms, and she had to stand on her tiptoes as she sought more, devouring him. As if reading what she needed, he bent lower, accommodating the height difference, and she moaned, relaxing into a more leisurely kiss while her hands skimmed his back.

Lean muscles streamlined him, and she indolently parted her lips, inviting him farther inside.

All male, she thought, missing the feel of one: the harder, rougher touches, the bigger hands and the wider chests. But she loved getting to know a new man even more…

His tongue explored her, slowing their tempo until he

withdrew to press small kisses to the tip of her mouth. Her jaw. Her neck.

Carmen opened her eyes, the overhead light blurring and burning into her. She moved with every gentle buss, grasping his shirt until it bunched in her hands. And when he sucked her earlobe into his mouth, she fell against him, her breasts crushed into his chest.

Her nipples pebbled at the contact, and their sensitivity made her weaker, even as she grew stronger.

This is way better than I remember, she thought cloudily. *A first kiss. Shouldn't it be more awkward? Sloppier? Shouldn't—*

A knock on the door wedged them apart.

"Hey, lovebirds?" a male voice said. "I gotta go."

Carmen's hand absently went to her hair. It felt mussed up, and she realized that Eddie had been lulling her by running his fingers through it. She hadn't even been aware—not with everything else that'd been going on.

"I guess seven minutes is up?" she asked.

"I think it was a while ago."

Eddie took her chin between his thumb and index finger. When their eyes met, he looked at her— No, *in* her.

The penetration shook her, but maybe that was only her body reacting to the aftermath of their kiss.

"You've been the highlight of this trip, Carmen," he finally said.

"You just started."

"And, believe me, before this afternoon, I was ready for it to end."

Again, she wondered just why he was with his friends if he wasn't enjoying himself.

"But," he continued, "we're off to Lake Havisu tomorrow.

There's a houseboat we'll be using and it wasn't ready today. If you want to come…"

He left the option hanging, and impetuously, Carmen wanted to grab it, to see what tugging on it might unleash if that kiss was any indication.

"Maybe I'll check with Lucy," Carmen said. She had already gotten *her* way today with the Vegas cancellation, and it wasn't fair to her friend to demand more. "I've already asked a lot of her."

As more people knocked on the door, Eddie bent down to give her one last, lingering kiss. It tingled on her lips, even when he pulled back.

"Try to persuade her?" he whispered.

Then, as he turned around to unlock the door, he slayed her with that grin.

Yow. Za.

He opened the door, revealing two of his friends: the blond curly-haired girl and Richie, the birthday boy. After a strange look at Eddie, who ignored her, Blondie bolted past them and shut the door as soon as they crossed the threshold.

Glam-rock music filled the room while they avoided Richie's low "whoo-whoo" whistle, instead making their way back to the dwindling party. The strawberry-blond girl with Lindsay Lohan freckles—Carmen had only noticed thanks to Lucy—was stretched out on a bed with a pillow over her head. One of the guys lounged beside her. The remaining two were chatting at the Quarters table, the game abandoned.

But, much to Carmen's shock, they had another guest.

Lucy was sitting at the table, too, her hair tousled, her skin flushed, her eyes glowing.

And, most curious of all, her smile loopy.

"Lucy?" Carmen asked.

Her friend's smile widened, and she let out a laugh that made Carmen wonder what the hell had happened in Lucy Land tonight.

AFTER SEX with the cowboy, Lucy had been bursting with crazy energy, so without wasting any time, she'd hoofed it back to the party, dying to share what she'd done.

Carmen would never believe it. And maybe hearing the story out loud would even convince Lucy that she'd broken a lamp while doing the dirty with a mysterious cowboy.

Her friend had taken one look at Lucy then hustled her back to their room where the entire story unfolded. Afterward, the other woman had looked at Lucy as if she'd lost her mind.

And maybe Lucy had.

Even now, Carmen sat on her bed, openmouthed.

Lucy shifted. Yup, she'd had sex with a man whose name she didn't know.

Long live the new Lucy—a woman who *could* damn well walk away instead of the opposite scenario.

"Where did you…meet this cowboy guy?" Carmen asked.

Lucy couldn't help but notice that her friend had some finger-tousled hair going on herself, but she saved her own questions until later.

"The diner," Lucy said. "I mean…we kind of talked. In a way. Sort of."

"What does *that* mean?"

A laugh burbled out of Lucy. This was nuts. "He overheard Eddie inviting us to the motel and, while I was in the gift shop, thought to warn me about hooking up with strangers. Ironic, huh?"

Carmen closed her eyes, clearly still processing everything. "So you actually chatted for a few minutes with this…what's his name?"

"I don't know."

The other woman's eyes almost bugged out of her head. "I thought you might be just kidding about that part."

"Nope."

As Carmen rested a hand against her forehead, Lucy added, "It's not like it'll matter. Remember what you told me earlier, in the car? How you made that stranger fantasy seem so appealing? Well, it sure turned out to be."

"I just…" Carmen waved her hands around. "I never expected this from you. You never even said anything about him in the car."

"He'd mentioned he was staying here, but nothing like this ever happens to me, so I kept my trap shut."

"But it did happen to you." Carmen paused. Then the situation seemed to hit her all at once, and she laughed, coming over to sit on Lucy's bed. "You little pixie, you. Was it everything you ever dreamed of?"

In spite of Carmen's light tone, Lucy's body flared, as if heating with the imprints of his hands and lips on her skin. She could still feel his erection filling her up, thick and hard.

"It was…more," she said. "You know, regular sex is so run of the mill, I suppose. You go out a few times, kiss, build up to the big moment, and it's all very good, but…" She flapped a hand in front of her warming face. "Then there's tonight's sex."

And then there was *her*, Lucy Christie, the girl who wore conservative skirts to work every day and knew her company's human resources manual backward and forward. She'd gone crazy in the heat, and it'd happened faster than she could've ever imagined.

Her cooped-up id had finally come out to play.

Carmen took a pillow out from under the bedspread and hit her friend with it. "So what did he look like? I've got to know the juicy details."

"Why? You look like you could tell me some yourself."

"Oh, babycakes, I've got nothing on you. We'll save my story for after."

So Lucy went into the gentler details, keeping the more intimate ones for herself. All the while, Carmen listened, an intrigued expression on her face.

When Lucy finished, she tossed the pillow back at Carmen. "Now you."

"Me? I'm an amateur in the presence of a sex goddess."

"Come on, surely you and Eddie…"

Carmen sighed and leaned back against the headboard. "A kiss. Can you believe it? After all my big-girl blather… And the thing was, I was scared to death."

Lucy widened her eyes.

"No joke," Carmen added. "When it came right down to it, I realized that I haven't played the field and… Man, now that I think more about it, I suppose I could've been nervous that I might be a terrible lover and that's why Malcolm had cheated."

"But you know that's crap now?"

"From the way Eddie seemed to enjoy kissing me? Um…yeah." Something changed in Carmen's eyes, a shift in thought. "I can't believe this, but I think a kiss might've made me feel better than full-on sex could have."

Lucy just sat there, wondering how that might be possible after the night she'd had.

Then Carmen sat up. "But that's silly. Kisses are romantic and sex is sexy. And I'm not on the market for a romance, just a little nookie. Who needs to be tied down again."

"Carm, I'm sorry I took you away from Eddie." Lucy nodded toward the door. "You going back?"

Her friend got off the bed and went for her suitcase, opening it then grabbing an oversize SDSU T-shirt. "No, I think the party was winding down anyway. I'm fine with what I got…for now."

Lucy waited for the follow-up.

And, indeed, while Carmen changed into her nightshirt, she explained about Eddie's houseboat and Lake Havisu. Even before she'd finished, Lucy knew what they should do next on their revised road trip.

"Seeing as I cut off your courting dance by blasting in there with my tale of tail," Lucy said while Carmen went to the sink and brushed her teeth, "I think we should spend some time on the lake. We can cancel our other reservations and play everything by ear."

Besides, Lucy thought, she wanted Carmen to come away from their vacation satisfied, too.

She dwelled over that word: *satisfied.* Was she? No, not really. Her body cried out for more.

Because the more she got, the more independent she was bound to feel.

Over by the sink, Carmen did a happy dance at the new arrangement. Glad to see it, Lucy hopped off the bed to get herself nightified, as well.

Then she noticed something sticking out from under the pillow Carmen hadn't disturbed. It looked like money, tucked under the crease of the pillow and bedspread.

Money?

She pulled it out as Carmen went into the bathroom.

Three faded twenties.

Lucy could only stand there. Had the cowboy left this? And what did it mean?

Her glance coasted to the broken lamp on her nightstand—she and Carmen had enjoyed a good laugh over that when they'd first come in the room—and she wondered if maybe her one-night fling was merely paying for the damage. He'd told her he wanted to.

However, even though she was sure that's what the money was for, she hid the bills in her purse so Carmen wouldn't see them.

It was only another detail she wanted to keep to herself.

Another part of a fantasy that was growing by the heartbeat.

5

THE NEXT MORNING over biscuits and gravy in the near-empty coffee shop, Lucy and Carmen talked about what they might want to do beyond Lake Havisu. Lucy was still getting used to this fly-by-the-seat-of-your-pants approach to life, and even if she ended up throwing out this particular list, it gave her a measure of direction.

But the fact that she *could* throw it out only added an element of excitement to the next couple of weeks.

"After you get what you want from this Havisu houseboat trip," Lucy said, "there's Oatman. It'd be the closest I'll get to anything cowboy again."

She wasn't quite ready to leave him behind, even though the money niggled at her. She'd even been hoping to see him in the coffee shop one last time, just so she could give the bills back. She earned enough money to be comfortable, and she didn't like accepting any—especially with all its paid-by-the-hour echoes.

"Oatman," Carmen repeated. "We could go the tiny-Western-town route. I read in the guidebook that they stage gunfights there."

She'd taken the booth seat facing the door, and Lucy knew it was because her friend was hoping Eddie might come through.

Both of them were *so* in heat.

"Oatman's not too far away from Lake Havisu City." Lucy paged through the guidebook, coming to a map that she'd highlighted with their original route. She ignored the yellow line in favor of seeking out new options. "We'll see what happens though, okay?"

Carmen wiped her mouth with the napkin, grinning at Lucy. "Okay. And, Luce?"

"Yeah?"

"Thank you."

Lucy shrugged it off, indicating that gratitude wasn't necessary. She was pumped about seeing what was in store for them, and she hoped it included some action with Eddie for Carmen.

But for Lucy, herself?

Well, for now she would hold on to her cowboy fantasy because the novelty of it was still feeding her with ideas about what else she would change when she got home. Her job?

Yeah... Why *was* she chaining herself to something she didn't enjoy?

While trying to find an answer, Lucy settled the bill with Carmen, then prepared to move on. Her friend posted a quick blog on the office's rental computer, and Lucy made arrangements to check out and pay for the damaged lamp. Then, after they climbed into their car, Lucy took a moment to appreciate their vehicle.

To appreciate where she was and where she might be going.

Previously, she'd merely been playing a wishful role—the girl on a nostalgic road trip—by borrowing this car from her brother. A red 2005 Mustang convertible with its retro-designed red leather seats and black highlights. But now, she felt as if she *belonged* in something so spirited.

"And...we're off," Lucy said, starting the engine.

But she didn't head for the motel exit. Not yet. Instead, she drove the opposite way.

"Where…?" Carmen started to ask.

But she must have realized that Lucy wanted to cruise the motel, looking for signs of the cowboy. There'd been a beat-up red pickup near the office, as well as a gold SUV, but she couldn't be sure either of them belonged to her stranger. So what should she do—knock on doors to find him?

Dissatisfied, she headed for Eddie's motel room.

If neither of those vehicles were his, maybe her cowboy had left right after the sex, Lucy thought. Or maybe he was restless like her, wanting an early start on the day.

Whatever it was, Carmen was in luck. Eddie's subdued group was outside, clearly hungover. The guy himself was out there, too, dressed in jeans and a Henley with the sleeves rolled up his straining forearms to his elbows. He was the only person in the group moving with fluid grace while packing one of two cars—an old blue Cadillac. The other was a black Ranger.

After stopping, Lucy allowed the engine to idle, and Eddie glanced up, a smile spreading across his face when he saw Carmen.

Lucy elbowed her friend, cueing her to say something. Odd—nothing usually got confident Carmen's tongue.

Finally, the other woman managed to talk. "Looks like you're packed for a long voyage."

Her object of lust leaned against the Caddy, all laconic ease as he watched Carmen.

Then one of his friends—the guy she'd come to call Roy Rogers—came out of the room with a garbage bag of clothes in hand. He waved at Lucy, looking ashen yet cheery.

"Yo, Lucky!" he said. "Back to see me?"

College kids. Oh, how clueless they all were at that time in their lives.

"Dare to dream," Lucy answered.

But Carmen only had eyes for Eddie. "I guess," she said to him, "we'll see you on the docks."

"You've got my number," he said.

"Yes, I do."

Knowing a good closing when she saw one, Lucy gunned the engine and took off, around the motel and back toward the exit.

Giving each other conspiratorial grins, they put on their sunglasses and hit the 40, heading for I-95, which veered toward the lake. All the while, Carmen couldn't wipe her own smile from her face, and Lucy knew exactly how her friend felt.

Finally.

But thinking of her night with the cowboy only got her riled up as the wind messed with her ponytailed hair. She kept feeling his hands on her thighs, his mouth kissing her in the most private of places…

Lucy was lost in hazy near delirium until they got to their exit. Truthfully, she was lucky they didn't crash into anything.

But, once on the new highway, Carmen raised her hands in the air, her short hair almost standing on end in the full breeze. "I'm robbing the cradle!"

They laughed, both of them obviously addicted to what last night had ushered in. Some might define a one-night stand as tawdry—even the old Lucy might have—but now that'd she'd done it, she could only call the experience enlightening.

And if she could, she would do it again. And again. And…

They whooshed past cacti and sand, but it all blurred together. She'd gone back to thinking about stubble burn and heavy breathing, reliving every moment, every caress.

She barely even saw the RVs they were passing or the mileage signs coming and going. It was only when a battered red pickup zoomed by them, then slowed after pulling in front, that Lucy blinked herself out of it.

Was it the truck from the inn?

"I think he's checking you out, Luce," Carmen said over the wind. "Another cowboy to add to your list?"

In the truck's rear window, Lucy saw a weathered hat that resembled the stranger's, and her belly clutched.

It was him—she knew it.

Then the driver sped off until his vehicle became a vanishing pinpoint on the silver ribbon of road.

She put pedal to the metal, wanting to catch up to the truck, but the car's temperature gauge began to rise, and she eased off. By that time, the truck was too far gone.

Something inside Lucy sank. Disappointment. An opportunity to expand her horizons, to put more curves between her and the straight lines she'd always followed.

But she couldn't complain this time—it couldn't have ended more perfectly. *She'd* done the leaving last night, not him, and it was a beautiful change of pattern. That had to count for something.

Didn't it?

"Well, look who finally arrived," Carmen said.

The Ranger and Caddy pulled ahead, their tempered speed slowing Lucy down. That was no doubt a positive thing. And when someone held up a sign in the back window of the Cadillac, Lucy grinned at their antics.

We'll Have A Lot More Than Seven Minutes, it said, a simple message that made Carmen look out the passenger window, hiding her expression.

Then the two vehicles sped ahead, hell-bent for leather.

Lucy waited for Carmen to remark on the sign, but she didn't. Instead, the wind continued its tune and they stuck to the speed limit. They were close to the lake anyway.

When they came upon it, an English village stood guard over the channel's shore and London Bridge stretched over the early-afternoon water. Lucy had read that the town purchased the structure in an auction during the early seventies, and it was the real deal. Walking its length would be an item to check off a trip to-do list, she thought.

If she still had one—

Wait.

She parked and cut the engine. Why *did* she need lists? What good did they really do?

Carmen's phone rang, and when she answered, it was obvious that Eddie was calling. As they planned to meet, her friend blushed.

Blushed.

It was a first, and Lucy wondered just what was going on with Carmen besides all the strangers-make-for-good-sex talk.

Her friend hung up. "He's going ahead to see to the houseboat, and the rest of the group is grabbing an early lunch at a microbrewery in the village. Want to go there?"

"Why not? Carm?"

"Uh-huh?"

Lucy wanted to ask a thousand questions, but none of them came easily. Wouldn't Carmen volunteer to tell her what was on her mind? Lucy shouldn't have to ask.

"It's nothing," she finally said. Her friend would talk about it if she wanted to. Besides, *she* hadn't even told Carmen everything about last night…

They got out of the car, mild, dry heat enveloping Lucy. The aroma of barbecue traced the air, too, and she stretched, taking in all the boats dotting the water, all the spring-break school kids and families milling about on the walkways. Then they headed toward the Elizabethan English village.

But something Lucy saw out of the corner of her eye stopped her.

The red truck from the motel, parked in a sparsely populated area of the lot.

She looked closer, her pulse quickening. There was a man behind the wheel, his Stetson drawn low over his face.

Her cowboy.

As her blood raced, she put her hand on her purse, remembering the money in there.

"Lucy?" Carmen asked, waiting up ahead.

He opened the door and climbed out of the truck, and Lucy got a rush so powerful that she couldn't move.

"It's him, Carm," she said, mouth dry.

"Him?" Her friend's voice went high. *"Him?"*

"Quiet." Slowly, Lucy turned to the other woman. "How about I meet you real soon?"

Carmen hesitated, inspecting Lucy's object of lust, then raised a cautious finger. "Oh my God, he's hot. But I'm calling you in a half hour, Luce. You can always use it as an excuse to leave if things get out of control."

If only. "Okay."

And with that, Lucy gave her friend the please-go-now wide eyes and prepared to approach her cowboy.

JOSHUA DIDN'T WANT to hide from the brunette now, just as he hadn't when he'd passed her on the road back yonder.

So, as she walked across the parking lot, he leaned against the truck, one ankle crossed over the other, his thumbs hitched in the belt loops of his faded jeans. He would take whatever medicine was coming to him.

When she got near enough for him to read her sunglass-accessorized face, she didn't look frightened at his presence or even angry. Good. He didn't want to encourage either emotion but, damn him, he hadn't been able to help himself by chasing her down. She'd kept him awake all night, that woman, and it'd seemed like good old-fashioned serendipity when he'd stepped out of the motel office this morning to find the taillights of their slick car wheeling around to the other side of the complex.

He'd recalled the conversation from the diner: how the college pup had told the women that he and his friends were on their way to Lake Havisu. If Joshua was a betting man—and he used to be quite the gambler at the weekly poker runs he'd enjoyed with his neighbors—he would say that the women were off to accompany those college kids there.

So on this day when he didn't have anywhere to be, Joshua had found himself heading that way, too. He hoped to high heaven that this didn't mean he was a menace, but he would take that chance if it meant seeing her again.

The brunette had actually passed him on the highway once, but she'd acted as if she hadn't seen him underneath those cat-eyed sunglasses. Then he'd passed her, and he thought that maybe, just maybe, she recognized him that time.

Road games, he thought. A most welcome diversion from the reality of his shambles of a life.

As the brunette drew closer, her dark ponytail swayed as sinuously as her hips. She was dressed in a red-and-white checked sleeveless top and a white tennis skirt—innocent as a fifties siren.

Just as seductive, too.

As she came to a stop a few yards away, he tipped his hat to her. She barred her arms over her chest. Uh-oh. No games for her?

"So we meet again," he said.

"What a coincidence."

Behind her sunglasses, he imagined her deep blue eyes lasering into him. The heat cut through him, sizzling his skin.

Okay, maybe she *was* angry at seeing him here, and being raised by his dearly departed mom as a gentleman—most of the time, at least—he would have to respect that, like it or not.

"I'll leave if you're uncomfortable," he said. "It's not my intention to—"

She'd reached into her purse and extracted some money. Joshua recognized the amount of it.

"You left something at the motel." She held the cash toward him. "Needless to say, even if I charged by the hour, this sure wouldn't be enough."

Oh, good Lord. "That was for the lamp, ma'am, nothing more. I didn't mean to insult."

She leveled a low glance at him, edging down her sunglasses so he could see her eyes. There was a spark of glee in their depths, matching the emerging slant of her lips.

"Didn't I ask you not to call me ma'am?" she said.

Joshua wasn't sure where he stood right now. Yes, physically he was on the blacktop of a parking lot that he shouldn't have even dared set foot on, but he meant figuratively.

Was she just being saucy?

Was she…flirting?

Hope washed over him. The emotion was such a stranger that it took him a moment to identify it. Along with his land, he'd been robbed of that particular valuable, as well.

Yet, somehow, this woman managed to bring it back.

He grasped on to that hope before it was taken, too. "If I don't call you ma'am, what am I supposed to use?"

"Certainly not something that sounds like a bordello madam." She flapped the money, signaling that he should take the stuff.

He refused by holding up a calm hand. "I don't live under any debts, miss. You keep it."

"Miss?" She pushed her sunglasses back up, but it couldn't hide her amused expression. "Okay, miss will do. It's way better than ma'am. But, all the same, I can't accept your cash."

It was only sixty dollars, but it might go a long way on this fool's journey of his. As it was, he was stretching his wallet, especially after the loss of his family's property.

The brunette pushed the money at him again, jutting out her hip. She had no idea what she was playing with here.

"I won't take the cash back," he said flatly.

She lowered her arm, then tapped the bills against her thigh, staring at him.

Then she smiled, and he was so taken that he couldn't help doing the same. How did she manage to make him forget so easily?

"Seems we're at an impasse then," she said.

"Seems so."

"I suppose I'll have to think of a good way to get rid of this money without actually spending it."

"All right, all right, if hanging on to it makes you feel dirty somehow, then—"

"I wanted dirty," she interrupted.

The reminder of last night hit him full force. The muscles lining his belly jerked, escalating a hunger nothing could assuage right now except her.

"I guess," she said, taking a step closer, "you just like to feel in control by shelling out the bucks. That's why you don't want them back. Am I right?"

His body went tighter in primitive response. "Everyone wants control in some manner."

And maybe leaving that money had been a small way of taking it back when she had made it clear that she was done with him for the night. Lord knew he'd lost enough control with the ranch and then her. If he could just get both of them back…

"Maybe if you told me your name, I'd be a mite easier to work with," he said. Her name would mean that he'd at least won a bit of her, and that was a start.

"Why's it so important for you to know?" she asked. "Because I'll tell you something—names have no part of this."

He straightened. "This? What's *this?*"

She seemed caught off guard at the question, as if she had no idea how to answer. Then she smiled.

"*This* is why you ended up here at Lake Havisu when I doubt it was on your agenda. *This* is why we're both standing here when I could be inside drinking beer with my friend while you…I don't know, brood in your pickup or whatever."

Joshua chanced a cocky smile, starting to understand what she wanted from him. "No strings attached, right? You're a girl on vacation and that's all you were looking for last night."

"And then you showed up here, screwing up my escape plan."

Her own cheeky smile told him that he'd walked right into her fantasies.

Well then. They could stand here all day talking like polite strangers or he could come out with what was obviously on both of their minds.

"What're your plans for the day...*miss?*"

"What are yours?"

Yup, cheeky.

"I had a couple of ideas in mind," he said.

He saw how her fingers clutched at her skirt, the only sign that she was hesitating, that maybe she wasn't as naughty as she came off. That's when he recalled her sunshine-on-the-horizon smile and how it reminded him so poignantly of home, of what had been broken...

As his heart ached, he wondered if he even missed more than the stolen land. If his protectiveness of the whole ranch was a sign that his feelings ran deeper than he realized.

But in the next instant, the brunette was back to raising her chin and giving him a saucy look, and he wasn't sure what the hell was what.

She emphatically took her phone from her purse then dialed and held it to her ear.

"Hey, Carm, it's me," she said, gazing at him all the while, setting him on sexual edge. "Something's come up, and it's wearing a cowboy hat. Yes, *yes,* but would it be okay if I met you in..."

Vision going passion-bleary, he held up two fingers. It was going to take at least a couple of hours to make up for all the sleep he'd lost over her last night.

Her lips parted at the number he suggested. Then she recovered, cool as ever. "Are you sure you're okay with this?"

After a pause, she laughed at whatever her friend said in return. "Right. Then have fun, and we'll keep in touch. Bye."

Slowly, she folded her phone and put it away. Then she glanced at the cash she still held in her hand.

"I have a proposition," she said.

Joshua's body was already revving, a machine set into motion at the carnal images roaring through his brain. Flesh memories of her long legs under his palms, his fingers slipping between her sex...

"Name it," he said.

She nodded toward his truck. "How roomy is it in there?"

He opened his door. "Roomy enough."

"Okay." She sidled toward him, wedging the bills between her index and middle fingers. "I'm going to give you a shot at getting what you want."

Lust planked him. "Your body?"

"If you're lucky. I'm talking about something else. Something you've asked me for a few times now."

Her name?

"I'm guessing," he said, leaning closer to her until his words rustled the fine, stray hairs near her ear, "that I'm going to have to work to know who you are."

She shuddered, and he put his hand on the small of her back, unwilling to wait any longer to touch her. The contact seared his palm, marking him.

"You catch on quick." She turned her head slightly, lowering her voice. "Every guess you make about my name gets you a prize. However, if you don't get it right before my clothes are off, you're out of luck."

"Wait, there're a million names out there."

"I don't think you'll mind playing though." She rested a hand on his chest, and his heartbeat tripled in time. "Take your first guess now."

His breathing went shallow. She was tart yet sweet beneath it all. She was hot yet cool. An enigma. What kind of name would she have?

He had no idea, so he threw one out there. "Based on blue eyes, dark hair and paradoxes alone, I'll say Angelina."

"Ooooo, an angel's name for the media's most questionably devilish woman." She took off her sunglasses and slid them into her purse. "But…wrong. Although I do appreciate the thought."

Her electric-blue eyes bore into him and he couldn't stop himself from pressing her against his hardening groin.

Sucking in a breath, she paused, as if overcome.

"Why do we need all these games?" he asked, voice gritty.

But she ignored him. "Guess again, cowboy."

Damn her. "Jennifer."

Now he was being an impatient smart-ass.

Casually, maddeningly, she reached around to her ponytail and eased off the band that was holding it, then put that away, too.

As her wavy dark hair tumbled free, his penis strained against his jeans. Against *her.*

"I get it," he said. "For every wrong answer…"

"You get more of a peek. You really can't lose unless you win by guessing my name."

Yeah, like getting her naked could ever be considered a loss. The thought of her bare and beautiful urged him to take her by the waist and hoist her into his truck, where she scooted back across the vinyl seats, past the long stick shift and to her side of the cab. There, she manually rolled down the window partway.

"Truly roomy," she said, peering around. "Clean… And it smells like pine air freshener."

He got into the truck, slamming the door. He'd parked in a less frequented area of the lot, but there were still people coming to and from their cars. He and his miss would have to be quiet and discreet.

But when she lay the cash down on the dashboard and then propped her sandaled foot right next to it, assuming a sultry position, he wondered if that would be possible.

He caught a glimpse of pink panties and he all but blew apart.

"One more thing, stranger," she said. "If you get all my clothes off with your bad guesses, then you get that dirty money back, too."

She smiled, probably already thinking she'd won.

6

THE CONTINUATION of a fantasy. Sex with a stranger.

That's what she wanted from him: no small talk, no wooing and definitely no names.

Besides, she doubted he would guess hers. How many people nowadays were named something old-fashioned like Lucy anyway?

She moved her bent leg, which was propped on the dashboard, back and forth. That caught his eye.

He was all hers, and the power of that knowledge turned her on.

"Any more guesses?" she asked, provoking him even more by tracing her fingers along her inner thigh.

She saw his Adam's apple work in his throat. Oh, she was being a real bad girl, toying with him like this.

Who would've guessed she had it in her?

He surprised her by slowly taking off his hat, smiling a secret smile, then putting his headgear in the window, as if to partially block what was about to go down.

"No one's around to see," she said.

"Maybe I'm just overprotective."

The way he said it gave her pause. Fierce, dead serious. His tone strayed too far from the amusing scenario she'd constructed.

So she pushed the game. "I'm waiting for your next guess...or don't you want to play?"

A predatory grin curved his lips, and her blood raced.

"All right then," he said. "Eliza. It's a soft name, but it also sounds like a genteel woman who craves action."

Lucy reached over to her dashboard-bound foot, slipped off her sandal then allowed it to drop to the floorboards. Lowering her leg, she anchored her bare foot near the stick shift, canting her knee against it, coyly inviting him without even saying a word.

"You aren't going to give me any hints, are you?" he asked.

Gosh, a girl might think he was more focused on getting her name than seeing her body. But, then again, every time she looked at him, she could see how much he wanted her.

"It's fewer than ten letters," she said.

"Great." He leaned an arm on the steering wheel, his muscles straining. Sleek under the tan of his skin. "That rules out something like Cinderella."

"I'll count that feisty comment as a guess."

She doffed her other sandal and rested that foot on the seat, parting her legs so that her skirt rode up to clearly show her undies.

His grin became even more wolfish, and he touched the red nail polish on her toe then traveled his fingers to her ankle, wrapping them around it.

"Fewer than ten letters," he said, massaging her with his thumb. "How about Tara? You look like a Tara to me."

At his every stroke, pressure thrummed between her legs, her clit swelling to a keen throb. She must not have been thinking straight, because the next thing she knew, she'd remarked, "You say that like you know a few Taras."

"Maybe there was one." He ran a thumb over her instep, making her jump. "Back in my wayward youth, before I realized that I preferred not sticking around for long, no matter what their names were."

Too much information. She didn't want him to think that she needed to know anything more, so she forged on.

"Next guess?" she asked.

"How about…Sheri? You look like you could be a sweet Sheri type in normal life."

He traced his thumb over the tender sole of her foot, and she bucked again, her clit seizing.

"Ticklish?" he asked.

Sassily, she tugged away from him. Then she reached up to her ear and removed one of her plain diamond earring studs.

"Aw, earrings count?" he asked as she set the jewelry in a cup holder near the dash.

"We've got two hours. Gotta stretch this out."

"I suppose we do." He went for her ankle again, but she moved farther away, just to be cruel.

"Next guess," she said, batting her eyelashes, totally out of control. Or way too much in it.

"At your command." He motioned toward the earring in the holder. "Just to get that other ridiculous ear accoutrement out and move this game along, my next guess is…Snow White."

Okay, fair enough. She discarded the other stud.

Then…an interruption.

A person was yelling and squealing outside the truck, and Lucy looked through the window. A laughing couple in bathing suits and flip-flops ran past in the near distance, the man chasing after the woman. When they reached a compact car, he pinned her to it, and they kissed, then opened the vehicle to get something out and leave.

The reminder that she and the cowboy weren't alone out here heightened the sexual stakes, thickening the air, her blood.

Her limbs went sensuously heavy with it, and she sank against the door, waiting for him to continue as adrenaline pushed her on.

"Next?" she asked.

He was ready. "Judy, Judith or any variation thereof."

The last word—plus his previous uttering of "accoutrement"—sounded strange coming from a cowboy. As she started to unbutton her blouse, she found herself wondering if he'd perhaps gone to college.

But that didn't mix with her fantasy. She wanted a simple lover with no complications, a rough-around-the-edges man who brought her that much closer to the elemental pleasure of discovering the woman who'd been buried inside her.

As if knowing what she needed, his gaze devoured her while she undid the clothing. Then, making the most of it, she gaped the material enough to give him a hint of her simple white lace bra. It gave her boudoir cleavage, made her feel feminine and sexy.

The sun slanted through his window, making his brown hair more golden, his eyes a hungrier shade of pale. She liked the way he looked at her, with no judgment. She didn't need to please him—only herself.

But best of all? She liked that she could leave at any time.

Inspired, she shrugged the blouse off her shoulders, and it skimmed down her arms. Her nipples beaded against the bra lace, and as she did away with her top, she slumped down in the seat, stretching her arms over her head. The position emphasized her breasts, showing them off to full advantage.

"Darlin'," the cowboy murmured, running a hand through his hair.

"*Definitely* not my name. Why don't you help me off with this skirt for that particular wrong guess."

He paused, then shifted forward. His hand flattened over her belly and forced her to suck in a breath. Her sex had tightened again, going plumper, damper.

With aching deliberation, he searched for the opening of her skirt, found it near her hip, undid the button, then the zipper. The friction of the sound wrested the air apart.

Even though the languorous process took him forever, it was worth the wait. When he was done, he tugged her skirt down her legs, discarding it on the floorboards and running his fingertips down her thighs.

Then he backed off, as if to give as good as he was getting from her—taunting and building the anticipation.

He hovered and, even though he was inches away, she could feel him on her flesh, a vibrating stimulation.

"Mary," he said, venturing another guess. "Common enough name. I've got to go with the odds."

Unable to break gazes with him, she shook her head.

"Bra," she whispered.

Reverently—how could she better describe it?—he unhooked her front clasp.

The cups parted, and he carefully peeled them away from her breasts. The air excited her nipples even more, or maybe it was the fact that his eyes were feasting on her again.

"Only one more chance to get it right," she said on the edge of a shiver.

As if in slow motion, she saw him start to form an L with his mouth, and she panicked. Hearing her name from him might ruin everything. Surely he wouldn't say—

"Laurie," he murmured.

Relief surged through her, infusing her with the confidence she'd lacked for an anxious moment.

She smiled, victorious. "Undies."

A hint of that darkness shaded him again—was her name really that important?—but it was overtaken by lust, pure and simple.

He placed his hand on her chest, then slid it between her breasts, making her rock upward as he continued down. Her stomach, her belly, her pubis.

Then he grasped her underwear with both hands and yanked it down, over her legs, her feet, freeing her of them.

"What now?" he asked, sounding as if his voice had been dragged through cut glass.

"You knew your way around me last night."

She didn't understand why, but he seemed to recall something about their encounter that needled him. She could tell by the sudden distance in his eyes.

"I get it," he said. "You're a player, and when you're done, you like to put the pieces back willy-nilly then stuff the box away."

She didn't know what to say.

But then some warmth eased back into his gaze, and he cupped one of her breasts, idly kneading it. She bit her lip, unable to talk anyway.

"It's just that I'm used to taking charge." He flicked a thumb over her nipple. "And that's not how it went last night at the end."

She was about to tell him to stop conversing, but when he took one of her legs and wrapped it around him, allowing him to get both knees on the seat, she sucked in a breath. Then he slid his hand to the junction of her legs.

Gently, he separated her already drenched lips, then coasted his thumb between them. Her hips automatically moved with his ministrations.

"I like to see what I can do for you," he added. "I like to see your face flush because I know that I made it happen."

Without warning, he inserted a finger into her, and she gasped.

"And I like to hear the sounds you make when you're pleased."

She moaned, wanting to please him right back, and he smiled at her satisfied response. Then he coaxed another finger into her, widening her passage, stretching her until she opened her mouth and uttered a tight cry.

She gyrated with his insistent rhythm, groping for a hold on the edge of the seat.

"Can you come for me?" he asked.

"Make me."

He used his other hand, his knuckle, to work her clit. As she grinded against him, she went blind, as if she'd gone out of body again, launched into a place where she was someone she hadn't fully become yet.

He kept going, pushing, urging, and she half whimpered, half groaned. It was the only sound she could hear in the echo chamber of her mind as she arched with the churning of his thrusting fingers.

Circling, building like a storm rising above the ground...

She zoomed along in the dark, rolling with every sensation. But when he lightly pinched her clit, he made her hit a wall.

She screamed, clutched at him as she threatened to blast apart.

But the pain felt so damn good, especially when she ricocheted off another wall, then another, finally blowing, fragments of her shooting up, falling…

A rain of ecstasy hitting the ground and forcing her sight to come back little by little.

She panted, vision clearing until she could see her cowboy above her, watching her meld back together in the heat of the air.

A stranger who had stayed, she thought, even when all the other men who'd made love to her had left.

A definite fantasy.

After a time, he withdrew his fingers, then stroked her legs, as if taming her. He looked so very content at having created her orgasm.

Soon, he reached down to grab her undies from the floor.

"You keep them," she said on a whim.

He laughed.

"Really." She pushed her damp hair back from her forehead. "Along with the money you just won, mister."

At the false name, his laugh dissipated, and he picked up her other clothes, helping her get back into them.

"How about a compromise then," he said.

She was just getting back into her shirt. It felt weird to go commando, but it felt wonderful, too, as if she'd accomplished something.

She'd joined the secret club of every happy woman who'd gone without panties, and it'd been quite the initiation.

"A compromise?" she asked.

"Yeah." He got behind the wheel and held up the money.

"What would you say to putting this toward our own room tonight?"

Miss No Undies shot her cowboy a big smile, wondering if she dared to go further.

EARLIER THAN EXPECTED, Lucy strolled into the microbrewery. She was on Sex Cloud Nine and had no doubt that it was obvious.

She found Carmen chatting with a few of the college kids in an atrium that overlooked the channel and London Bridge. They were nursing beers and snacking on baby back ribs, and when Carmen spotted Lucy approaching, she toasted her with a mug.

"Well, lookee here," she said, extending an arm so she could cradle Lucy into a welcome hug. At the same time, she stood and began to lead her friend away from the table. "What a rascal."

The Lindsay Lohan girl waved to Lucy, seeming happy to see her. At her side, the Roy Rogers clone said, "Hey, Lucky!" and Nickelodeon guy asked her if she wanted a beer.

Waving back, Lucy shook her head and thanked him. Meanwhile, Carmen guided her into a bar area, where the Yankees were playing on the TVs, then toward the restrooms.

"Back in the parking lot, when you were walking toward that cowboy, I watched for a few minutes," Carmen said, pushing open the door and ushering them inside the empty space. "Not long, but just enough to assure me that you had things in hand."

Lucy wasn't positive about who had been more in control during the parking-lot rendezvous. All she knew was that her skin still felt flushed, as if the stranger's hands had made her blood rise and burn her from the inside out. She also felt exposed, her skirt barely covering what she'd always hidden with underwear before now. The air tickled her there, a constant reminder of him.

Carmen checked under all the stalls, then turned to Lucy when she found them empty. “So…you look very well fed, my dear.”

“We had a nice…chat…in his truck.”

“Chat. Is that the euphemism for hot sex?”

Knowing a query for more information when she heard one, Lucy revealed her so-called tête-à-tête, again stopping herself from going into the details, even though Carmen was always the first person she confided in. It seemed right to keep something to herself, just as she had last night.

A secret written down and kept in a closed box, Lucy thought. It belonged to her alone, so it was all the more precious.

Carmen leaned back against the counter. “Can I meet him at some point? Just out of utter curiosity.”

It was on the tip of Lucy’s tongue to say, “Sure, why not?” but she hesitated. Truthfully, she didn’t want to make any introductions. That would make him too real, not the figment of a more exciting life that was still too new to fully believe in.

Not yet, at least.

She tried to explain that to Carmen. Tried. But her friend only looked confused.

“I’m not leaving you out of anything,” Lucy said. “Really. But once you start introducing a guy to friends, that’s a step. Know what I mean? It brings the interaction to a new level, and that’s the last thing I want.”

“Luce, I just wonder if he’s a good guy or not. If he deserves you.”

“So says the lady who plans to meet up with her own stranger today.”

“Eddie’s not…” Carmen clearly didn’t know how to finish the sentence.

"What? Even though you still don't know much about him, he doesn't fit into the 'stranger' category?"

"I suppose. You've met Eddie, but I don't know thing one about this cowboy. What if he…"

Lucy fetched a piece of paper from her purse. Before she'd left her cowboy, she'd written his license number down. Texas plates, she'd noted, putting the information away so he wouldn't see what she was doing before he'd gone to the nearby resort hotel to get a room.

She'd only done it for Carmen's sake. And…okay, maybe to appease the responsible Lucy that still nudged at her every so often.

Handing the number to Carmen, who inspected it, Lucy glanced in the mirror and ran a hand over her loose, wild hair. Yeesh, she looked as if she'd been tumbled but good.

Sweet.

"And where's his name?" Carmen asked.

"I don't want to know his name."

"Lu—You still didn't get it?"

Lucy sighed. "I seem to remember a conversation I had with some redheaded girl outside Peggy Sue's yesterday. What did we talk about…? Oh, yeah. That strangers were the beauty of the road and we could drive away from them the next morning and it wouldn't matter. You don't happen to recall that discussion, do you?"

Lowering her head, Carmen hid her expression. But when she glanced back up at Lucy, there was genuine concern in her gold-flecked eyes.

"Touché," her friend said. "I was running my mouth. But I never, in a thousand years, thought you'd listen to my nonsense."

Whoa. The girl who was supposed to be busting out after

her breakup with Mal was actually the careful one here? The world had flipped upside down.

Lucy came to rest on the sink counter next to her friend. Their arms brushed and neither of them said anything for a moment.

Have I gone too far? Lucy asked herself. More importantly, when she returned to real life, would she look back in embarrassment on what she'd done on the road?

She thought of the surge she got every time the cowboy set eyes on her, touched her. How could a girl who followed someone else's rules for a profession ever regret *that?*

Suddenly, she realized that maybe there was even some buried resentment about her human resources job: often, she watched the clock at her desk, just waiting to get home.

Just another reason for change—if she would carry out the risk…

"The cowboy wants to spend the night with me," she finally said.

The mere thought washed needful quivers down her limbs, leaving goose bumps in their wake.

Carmen seemed to turn that over in her mind. "He's the one registering for the room?"

"Yes, and I'll keep on my toes," Lucy said. "But that's part of the turn-on—the perceived danger."

"You know that if you gave me the room number, I could probably find out his name from the desk clerk. If I did it cleverly enough."

"You've got my back, I know that." Lucy grinned in a preamble to changing the subject. Carmen was going out on a limb, too. "And what about with you? When's Eddie letting you on the houseboat?"

"Any time. That's what the kids say anyway."

Lucy laughed. "The kids."

"They're all nice. So lively and...open, I guess you'd say." Carmen smiled wistfully. "Eddie doesn't seem to fit in with them though, and I'm not sure why. He likes them well enough, but I can tell he'd rather be off on his own, taking pictures. And one of the kids said something...*off*...while we were eating ribs."

"What?"

Carmen pursed her lips, then, "Richie said that *Edward* is renting the houseboat. That's what they all call him, can you believe it? It sounds so formal. And when I casually started to ask if any of them were chipping in with money—because the way Richie worded it made it sound like the houseboat was Eddie's treat—the others shot him a look. You know, like, 'Shut up, man.'"

"Hmmph. You'll just ask Eddie about it though, right?"

"He's somehow managed to make me do all the talking so far, but sure. How much of a secret can it be?"

They glanced at each other. The contents of this whole trip would be a secret when they got home, so Carmen's question held a trace of irony.

At that point, Lucy's phone rang. She checked the ID screen to see a number from the woman covering for her at work.

"You're joking with me," she muttered, letting the call go to voice mail. She would check it after she finished talking with Carmen, then she would catch up with her brother to also let him know where she was staying and in what room.

She was horny, not completely dumb.

Carmen patted her own purse. "I've been getting calls from Malcolm. Totally avoiding them, too."

"Vacation isn't supposed to include ex-boyfriends."

"Agreed." Carmen rubbed Lucy's arm. "So you'll be careful tonight, keep in touch, meet me tomorrow?"

"You got it."

They hugged, then drew back. Carmen still held on to Lucy, peering at her, absolutely serious now.

"Have fun with that fantasy," she said.

Lucy winked at her friend, wished her the same, then left.

She headed to the car for some necessities, then the Shoreline Resort, where the cowboy said he would be meeting her in the lobby.

7

JOSHUA WATCHED the no-name brunette drop an overnight bag onto the carpeted floor and take a gander around their Mediterranean-style room. Sixty dollars hadn't gone far, yet that was okay. Money was the last thing on his mind right now.

It looked as if she had gone to her car and packed only what she might need for the night. Major baggage would've made things seem a little more settled, he guessed, and she didn't come off as the type who longed for that.

She turned this way and that, scanning the lake-inspired artwork, the carved teak trimmings, the entertainment center filled with a TV and drawers. With every move, her skirt rustled, reminding him of what she wasn't wearing beneath it.

Putting down the bag of snacks he'd picked up at the market, he rested a hand on his back pocket, where her panties waited. A memento.

"Up to your satisfaction?" he asked, wondering if, off road, she was used to fancy hotel rooms or more modest offerings like the Timberline.

"Perfect for an assignation." She turned around, shooting him an impish grin.

Right, he thought. He was here to bang her, and that was the extent of it. Why did he have to keep reminding himself?

Because that's what he was to her—a leave-behind lay. And

why not? At least she thought he did something so well that she had come back for more. It gave him a sense of value in the most primal way, making him forget about the call he'd received about a half hour ago.

One of his sisters, Melinda, had phoned to let Joshua know that they missed him, to assure him once again that they were going to get through this crisis in the end.

He'd been short with her, not wanting to hear platitudes. He should've seen Trent's lies coming from a mile away. He could've done so much more than losing his temper on Trent's doorstep.

Even though Melinda had meant well, the call had actually debased him, reminding him of his shortcomings.

Yet it had brought to mind—to *heart*—the ranch where his parents had sat in the cabin's family room, holding hands on the couch while watching TV.

This, in turn, made him think of the first time he'd seen the brunette in her simple dress, and *that* made him want her all the more. So much that he couldn't stop to think about the reason he was connecting her and his home so profoundly.

He closed the curtains, only leaving a slit for sunshine, and pulled a chilled bottle of French-Loire sauvignon blanc from the bag, then a bottle opener and plastic glasses.

"Thirsty?" he asked.

The brunette—damn it, he had to think of something to call her besides that—smiled, then wandered over to take a gander at the bottle's label. She smelled so tempting: as soft and soothing as the air near the creek that ran through the stolen land back home.

When she was done, he uncorked the bottle.

"Do you know your wines?" she asked. "I don't, even though I kind of pretend to when I go into the store."

His ears perked up at the tidbit. "I took a course in wine production when I was getting educated in agribusiness at Texas A&M."

"Hold on, no credentials necessary with me," she said, arranging their glasses on the table so he could pour. "Remember, the less we know about each other, the better."

Her cut-and-dried rule made him bristle. He didn't like to admit it, but she made him wonder if he was beneath her with his down-home ways, and maybe she felt she was slumming with him. College wouldn't exactly support the fantasy some women had about simple cowboy codes and riding the range, so maybe she wanted to keep his roughness intact.

Then again, her refusal to hear anything personal also appealed. After all, why not be with a woman who already thought he was as low as he felt nowadays? She accepted that about him. No judgment or hard questions involved.

But wasn't he better than how she might perceive him?

"You don't have to remind me of our rules again," he said, taking off his hat and tossing it onto a nearby chair. Then he produced a slab of Gouda as well as apples and strawberries from the bag. "You're just here for the night, then it's time to move on."

"Unless you catch up again."

He casually shrugged at being called on his determination to be with her. No skin off his back, because he was getting just what he wanted.

"I'm glad you did catch up though," she said, unwrapping the carton of strawberries.

For once, he thought, his risks had paid off. When he'd

chanced most of his savings, as well as his time and effort, back at the ranch, the outcome hadn't been as successful.

She went to the sink to wash the fruit, and he sliced the Gouda. Back when he'd taken business trips as a financial consultant for ag businesses around the state, he'd done the wine-cheese-fruit combination on women in upper-class hotels. But now with—damn it, what should he call her?—it wasn't quite the same.

He felt that, at any minute, she might stun him, just as she had last night, when she'd wiped her hands of him after they'd finished that mind-blowing screw.

After the brunette came back and offered him the basket of strawberries, he took one, carefully sliding it past her full lips. She seemed taken by surprise at first, but then closed her eyes, languidly biting into the fruit and making a pleasured sound, just like the one in the truck when he'd built her up to an orgasm.

He went hard at the thought, his groin pulsing.

As she ate the strawberry, its juice lingered on her lips, making them even more vivid. He bent down, then sipped from her, licking up every last drop.

When he pulled away midkiss, she laughed low in her throat, as if knowing that he was sexually baiting her.

She pushed him back into the chair, straddling him. "Just so you know, my friend thinks you might be dangerous."

For Pete's sake, did she want him to feed this little stranger fantasy of hers?

All right.

"Dangerous," he repeated, relishing the word and realizing he really *could be* dangerous to someone like Timothy Trent.

As if to chase away the darkness, he pushed up the

brunette's skirt so he could see her sex. The sight of it lit him up inside, causing his cock to stir against his fly.

Downy hair covering the most intimate part of her. He could even see a hint of pink, pink flesh.

She braced her hands on his shoulders, her breath coming faster.

"Is my friend right?" she asked. "Should I be worried about being with you?"

He only smiled, leaving her to fill in the blanks of her desires. Then, casually, he reached between her legs, stroking her, and she stifled a moan, as if not wanting him to hear. But she was getting damp, and that told him all he needed to know.

"Why are you here if it causes such concern?" he asked.

"Because..."

Something cracked through her gaze, and he couldn't properly read it. Indecision? Reality?

Are you here because you're not sure who you are anymore? he supplied for her. *Or maybe you only need an anchor that you can let go of after you've gotten what you want out of me...*

Joshua's world came to a standstill. He was talking about himself, not her. But he hadn't been doing a very good job of letting go—of his bitterness, his anger or this new addiction.

He stopped strumming her and rested his hand on her thigh instead while reaching over to grab his wine. Taking a deep swallow, he didn't even taste it.

The brunette—there, now the nickname sounded better, more distant—watched him, no doubt wondering why he'd abandoned their foreplay. But, hardly put off, she drank her wine, too, then picked up a piece of Gouda to feed him.

The cheese was creamy, a decent distraction while she shifted on his lap, her sex brushing his.

Sure enough, his jeans-bound cock reacted appropriately.

"And...we're off," she said with a laugh so sultry that he thought maybe she was a little devil sent to keep him away from home for all time.

He fought the hunger for her, but it was useless. He needed this woman, whoever she was, if only for the night. Then he would move on, finding another one to temporarily consume him, until either he got the results of the land survey or he was rational enough to go home.

"Just who are you?" he asked as she pressed against him, wiggling her hips provocatively, teasing his groin, as she put her wine back on the table.

"Only a girl on a holiday."

She leaned forward, her arms on either side of him while they rested on the top of the chair. Her dark hair curtained him as her forehead touched the top of his head, and all he could smell was soft, luscious perfume, powdery and erotic.

She moved her hips again, torturing him, and his hands slipped down to her bare ass, cupping it.

"Is this why you hit the road?" he asked. "For a string of sexual thrills?"

"Not at first." She ran her fingers over his shoulders, down his chest. "I was really going to Vegas. But then we got diverted and...you know the rest."

Yes, he did.

And when she brushed down to his penis, the story continued from there.

A story he truly didn't want to end.

AFTERWARD, LUCY LAY naked on top of the bedsheets, glistening with sweat that was going sticky on her skin. Lubrication from the condom they'd used lingered between her thighs, and she pressed her hand against herself to feel the slip and slide of it covering her nether lips.

Oh…

She thought of him while touching herself. He was in the bathroom, with the water running in the sink, and she imagined him in the mirror, his brown hair wet with sweat, his skin ruddy with the same fever that addled her.

Part of her wanted to stay, just as she always found herself doing in the afterglow. Wasn't there some womanly chemical that made a female want to cuddle?

Well, Lucy didn't need it. Never again.

She heard the door open and stretched her arms above her head, elongating her body. Then he appeared, skin bare, the afternoon sun peeking through a slit in the curtains to shower gold over him.

God, he was gorgeous: muscles cording him together, his belly flat, his penis thick and nested in darker curls.

He caught her perusal. "You going to kick me out of the room now?"

"Not a chance."

She rolled to her stomach and propped a pillow under her chest as he crawled onto the mattress, lying on his side. With him, she didn't mind her nudity. She'd been a more modest creature before, but that was only because she hadn't been sure of herself.

Not a problem with him.

He rested his palm on the back of her thigh, then leisurely traced up to her butt. She gathered a second pillow and rested her head on it.

This was the part where they were supposed to talk in the

intimate hush. Thing was, with all her fantasy-required rules, there wasn't much to say—not if she didn't want to know anything about him.

The lack of discussion made her a tad anxious. It gave old Lucy too much time to think about what new Lucy was doing.

"You travel much?" she asked, settling on a neutral topic. "I mean, besides around this area?"

He kneaded her butt cheek, his fingertips inching between her thighs. Oh, he was killing her.

"I've done my share of living out of a duffel bag," he said. "Mainly in Texas. Business."

It always seemed as if he wanted to mention personal details. Boy, sex itself was so much easier than what came after.

"And how about pleasure?" she asked, getting back to the basics. "Where do you travel for that?"

A phone rang, and it took a second for her to realize that it was hers.

Thank goodness—saved by the cell.

"I'll bet that's Carmen," she said, getting out of bed. The shape of his hand lingered in heated remembrance on her rear end.

"Your friend, right?" he asked.

A point for the cowboy, Lucy thought, nodding. He'd gotten his tidbit of information, and he looked rather pleased at that while he rolled to his back and slid his hands beneath his head.

She fumbled her phone out of her purse, turned on by the sight of the hair under the pits of his arms. She thought that was sexy on a guy—earthy.

"Carm?" she croaked, then cleared her throat.

It didn't help that he was scanning *her* naked body, smiling as if he was doing wicked things to her in his head.

"I'm interrupting, right?" Carmen said. "Luce, I'm so sorry—"

"Not to worry. How're you doing?"

"Okay. I mean, Eddie isn't back yet, so I've been shopping with Sarah, the girl who you said looks like Lindsay Lohan. But this chick is together. She's a marine biology major at UCSD. Smart cookie."

Disappointment for her friend took over. "Where's Eddie?"

"I guess he needed to take care of some kind of business that must not be named out loud. No one wants to talk about it though, so I'm wondering what's up with the guy."

Eddie's mysteries continued to grow. Funny, how Lucy had a stranger who wanted to share more than she would let him and Carmen's seemingly open guy wasn't so forthcoming after all.

"Carm, I'll be there in—"

"Nope. No way. I'll be on a houseboat cruise before you can get your clothes on, okay? I just wanted to check in."

Lucy had called Carmen with her room number before, so they were set on that point. "Are you sure? This is our trip, after all."

"I'm positive." Someone in the background—Sarah?—yelled to Carmen. "Oop, see, we're going to meet Eddie at the boat now. Call me if you need to."

"I will. Have fun. Don't do anything—"

"Don't even say it, Luce." A trace of concern still marred her friend's tone.

But when they signed off, Lucy was so focused on the cowboy crooking his finger at her in bed that common sense flew out the window.

She put the phone back in its proper place as he spoke.

"Your buddy's off on her own adventure?"

"Houseboating."

"Then you're responsible for your own amusement, I take it."

"For the time being."

Lucy came back to bed to find him looking thoughtful. But when she brushed her knuckles against his penis, stirring it awake, he grinned, all else apparently forgotten.

He scooped her against his long, hard body and her mind turned to mist, taken over.

After they finished another bout of blood-churning sex, it took her a while to comprehend her surroundings, the room around her, the words he was saying as he kissed her neck.

"Huh?" she whispered, on the edge of a moan as he nipped at her skin postorgasm.

Then he locked gazes with her, his eyes a pale, fierce silver that cut through her fogginess. He was still hard inside of her, and he gave a thrust, working her right back up into an escalating glow.

"Why not have an even bigger adventure—" another thrust "—with me."

And, as he rolled to his back, taking her on top of him, she wasn't sure what her answer was, even though she was thinking, *Yes.*

Hell, yes.

HE EXPLORED her body—every sweat-slicked plane, every valley. He worked her, hitching her legs until they rested on top of his shoulders, buffeting her until she slid over the side of the bed and arched to the floor.

They were all over the place as he sought more than he'd ever needed, coming hard into her and pulling her back on the mattress to him, where she slumped to his chest in panting relief.

Joshua buried his face against her shoulder, breathing her in, tasting her sweat and skin. What he'd uttered right before they'd gone at it again dogged him.

Why not have an even bigger adventure with me.

He hadn't meant to say it. Not out loud, anyway. But she'd gotten that phone call from her friend, and all kinds of stray ideas had taken root in him. Foreign, colorful notions, like making her come for him on different beds in different places.

Nothing serious, he thought, just another game.

Another challenge.

He wanted to see how far she would go. Wanted to see how much *he* could take during some kind of masochistic test that could only make him stronger.

She pulled back from his mouth now, still straddling his body, her fingers lightly braced against his chest. Damn it, she hadn't forgotten his suggestion. That was clear from the questions in her gaze.

"Did you mean it?" she asked, breath straining in the flush of their intimacy. "A bigger adventure?"

What to do…backtrack? But he realized that he yearned to push the envelope with every energized fiber in him.

"I'm not talking about flying off to Paris or going on some safari in Kenya, now." He skimmed a thumb over her nipple, loving how it hardened for him. "I'm thinking of a mere jaunt. The same hotel room can get claustrophobic."

She inspected him with those summer-deep eyes, and the fact that she hadn't turned him down yet jolted a thrill to his very core.

"Oatman isn't a far trip," she whispered.

Oatman. He circled her nipple, and she shifted, closing her eyes slowly, then opening them.

"There's a hotel there," she added, "where Carole Lombard and Clark Gable had their honeymoon. Haunted, they say."

"Ever wonder what it'd be like to make it in a bed with a ghost around?"

She trembled, and he didn't know if it was because she was faking a scare or because he had gently pinched her nipple.

Her reaction delighted him beyond reason, and Joshua had never laid claim to that word before: *delighted.* It was too light, optimistic, carefree. But here he was using it.

As she pushed her hips forward, begging for more, greed took him over. Greed for her.

At that moment, his real reason for asking her to run off with him bared itself. He fed off her sex, her energy, her mystery. And until he'd tapped all of that out, he would be a glutton for her.

Often enough at home, he'd heard neighbors and childhood friends talk about addiction to a woman, but Joshua had been above it all—he'd known that no lady would ever obsess him, and no one had.

Until now.

But why? What exactly was it that fulfilled him when it came to her?

She'd blindsided him, taken him completely by surprise. And he had no notion of how to deal with it, especially since she wasn't the typical female who wanted to talk all the time and take more of him than he was willing to give.

Thing was, after their intimacy, he felt the urge to share. Yet he didn't dare. His situation was too humiliating, and it was best that he kept it to himself, as she obviously wanted him to.

The liaison should've been perfect for him, so why did he find himself needing more?

"Oatman," he repeated, as if he was still thinking about it. But he'd already decided.

A pulse throbbed in his neck, marking the passing seconds.

In the interim, she sank to the mattress on her back next to him. Then, as if lost in thought, she absently twirled a strand of her hair, and he couldn't help thinking that she did the same thing to him: winding him around a finger.

This could only come to no good. But he would worry about that afterward.

He sat up, took off the condom, disposed of it and came back to bed.

"The town started as a mining tent camp," he said, filling the silence, "then grew when there was a gold strike. But in the twenties, there was a fire, and soon after that, the big mining company closed. But the town attracted people from Route 66, and it managed to survive."

"And how do you know so much about it?" she asked.

Joshua grinned. It was his turn to withhold information. Yeah, he could play her game, too.

"Oh, so you're not going to tell me?" She lightly swatted at him. "No more dirty for you, cowboy."

But he knew she didn't mean it.

He could tell her the truth and clear the air if he really wanted to. After all, he'd only listened to a couple of old-timers at a roadside diner, and they'd told him about Oatman and other places on the Mother Road.

"Well, just so you don't feel too superior," the brunette said, propping herself up on her elbows, "I know a thing or two about the town, as well."

Her breasts weren't big, but they were firm and so nicely shaped. He couldn't take his eyes off them.

"What do you know?" he asked.

She seemed to like that he was visually feasting on her, and she turned to him, hardly bashful, even though he detected a faint hesitation, then a blush.

Damn, she was a puzzle.

"I know that there's a ghost called Oatie in the hotel, and that he's fond of hijinks. And that there're shops in town. I like shops."

"Don't most women?"

"No, not Carmen so much. She's the type who only goes to a store when she's forced to by circumstance or—" The brunette stopped herself, raising a finger. "You just lulled me into revealing something."

"You didn't reveal squat. I now officially know more about Carmen than you."

Bull. Even with the scant information she'd just given him, he felt as if he'd won an inch in the battle.

Content for now, he added, "I hear the Oatman Hotel is simple at best, but you can stay in that Gable-Lombard room."

A dreamy smile settled on her pink mouth, but then she grew more serious.

"You're thinking of your friend," he said. "She's going to be on that houseboat, right?"

"Yes."

"So we'll check out of here and be back by tomorrow night."

But he wondered if that would be enough.

"So…?" he asked, laying his proposition out there. "Do you want adventure or not?"

His no-name brunette turned to him, draping over his chest

so that her breasts crushed his skin. He automatically held her to him, wishing everything were this easy.

"Yes," she finally said, and he couldn't help noticing that there was a certain determination in her tone. "Let's do it, stranger."

8

ON A HOUSEBOAT floating on the serene surface of the lake, Carmen was concocting some *agua de melón* in the small kitchen, appreciating the new silence of a late afternoon.

They had finally headed out about an hour ago, after Eddie had returned. He'd been relatively distant as Sarah had thrown her arm around Carmen's shoulders and led her aboard, away from him, as if knowing he needed a buffer for some reason. The other kids had provided enthusiastic escort, too, and the party had started immediately.

Eddie hadn't been drinking though. In fact, aside from welcoming Carmen aboard soon afterward and telling her he intended to spend time with her as soon as he "wrapped up a few loose ends," he'd remained standoffish until he'd summoned the curly blond girl—Trudy—for a talk.

While everyone else got settled on the deck's lounge chairs, Carmen could barely hear Eddie's conversation from inside the cabin. Words were muted and even a little terse, but she had shamelessly caught references to a long phone call that Eddie had needed to make.

The discussion had ended when Trudy apologized to Eddie, came back to the group to grab a wine bottle, then headed for one of the bedrooms, alone.

"Looks like she claimed one early," Sarah joked. "Dibs on the second bedroom!"

Everyone started to lightheartedly argue over sleeping arrangements then, and Carmen had gone into the kitchen to find something nonalcoholic, as she wasn't really in the mood for spirits.

But Eddie had already disappeared, and she could hear his voice from the bedroom down the hall, forceful and maybe even a little angry.

She wasn't sure what to make of any of it. The only thing she knew was that Mal had kept secrets, too.

But wasn't Eddie a new chance? Had she even latched on to him in an odd effort to reinvent her history?

The rest of the kids stayed on the deck, fishing and drinking while Carmen concocted her drink. However, soon enough, the door down the hall shut and Eddie came to Carmen.

She nodded toward the blender. "Want some?"

He paused, as if taking in the scent of diced cantaloupe and watermelon. "Sure. Looks great."

"My mama's recipe, handed down from her own mom, whose own mother brought it over from Mexico."

For some reason, Eddie's forehead creased at her comment, but it happened so quickly that Carmen didn't remark on it.

"Your drink looks great." He rested a hand on his camera case, which waited for him on the counter. "Listen, I'm sorry I haven't been around much today. That wasn't the plan."

"Oh, no worries." She played it off, but it mattered. She'd been anticipating him—or more precisely, the *possibility* of him—all day. "Sarah kept me busy. She's interesting, with all her oceanic talk. And I didn't even mind shopping that much."

"Not your thing?"

She shot him a look. "I despise shopping. But we did need to go to the market, so it was inevitable."

As if to prove she'd actually been there, she swept her hand around the kitchen, indicating the fruit, veggies, booze and snacks they'd stocked up on.

Eddie nodded, slipping his hands into his jeans pockets, as if he wasn't sure what to say next.

Sighing, Carmen went to the sink, where she rinsed her hands and peered out the window. Outside, the kids sat on their chairs with their fishing poles and drinks.

"You don't want to be with them?" She turned off the water. "Because it strikes me that you're not exactly part of the crowd."

"I like them well enough. It's just…" He waved the rest of his comment away. "We weren't meant to vacation together."

Did that explain why she was getting these odd vibes about his relationship with the kids? Hardly.

"You take care of this crowd or something?" she asked. "I mean, I heard from a little birdie that you're paying for this houseboat, and you seemed rather guardianlike with Trudy."

A thought nibbled at her: she was trying to figure out what was going on between him and Trudy. There'd been the odd look she'd given him after they'd come out of the bathroom from Seven Minutes in Heaven at the Timberline Inn. Then there'd been this phone call today. And now his stern talk with the blonde in the bedroom.

Eddie turned away, taking his camera case with him. Almost reverently, he took the item out of its shelter and began adjusting it.

Why was it so hard to get any conversation out of this guy?

Suddenly, she felt lonely, even with him in the room. Why

she'd come on this boat, she had no idea. Sure, her hormones had driven her to follow Eddie Kilpatrick, but there was no better reason, unless you counted all her deep thinking about wanting to rediscover herself or…

Whatever.

She was out of place, out of sorts, and she had no cause to complain because it was what she'd wanted.

Drying her hands, she chastised herself for breaking off from Lucy. She missed her friend, but when she'd seen how Lucy had greeted that cowboy in the parking lot, she'd felt out of it there, too. And it wasn't Lucy's fault. Hell, no, Carmen didn't begrudge her pal even a second of fun.

But being here?

Only made Carmen feel older and more lost than ever.

Out of the corner of her eye, she saw Eddie aiming his camera at her, heard the shutter click and saw a flash shroud the room.

She held her hand up. "Don't waste your film."

"Why?" He held the camera away from his face. It was the happiest she'd seen him all day, behind the lens. "You're photogenic."

"And you're a liar." She smiled, pouring her blended melon and water into a pitcher, then adding more water and sugar. She didn't have the patience to chill the concoction, so she poured it over ice into two tall glasses.

"Let me take more pictures and I'll prove you wrong," he said.

Bringing his glass to him, she shook her head. "No dice."

"Carmen." His grin had gone killer again. "Trust me."

Trust him.

She backed away a step, holding her own glass with both hands, almost as if it were a shield. "I had enough problems trusting the guy who lied to me about seeing other women before we broke up. And you want me to trust *you?* The Eddie Kilpatrick who veils himself in an astounding lack of information?"

A tinge of what she thought might be sympathy clouded his eyes, but she wasn't sure. Maybe she didn't want it, so she wouldn't identify it.

"I don't know thing one about you," she said, "and you know all the embarrassing crap about me. I have no idea how that happened."

"Because you can't help but be trusting. I imagine that's what makes you a good person. Someone who attracts other people."

"Oh, smooth." Carmen toasted him with her glass. "You're a slick talker."

He braced a hand on the table, hunching forward, languid and persuasive. "The group loves you, Carmen. And I've been counting the minutes until *we* could be alone again."

Her heartbeat slipped from her chest toward her belly, beating there.

"You sure you're only twenty-three?" she asked. "Because you've got a whole lifetime of moves."

"Age is irrelevant." He straightened, as if uncomfortable with her observation. "Some people don't live at all, even after decades. I'm not going to be one of them."

Now, with this determination, he sounded young. It was a glimpse past his charming armor, telling her more than hours of conversation ever could. And she related. God, did she ever.

"Expectations," she said. Age was just another category people created for each other. They expected certain things out of twenty-year-olds, out of thirty-year-olds, and on and on. "I've been dealing with certain expectations my whole life, with my mama saying that I need to get married by such-and-such year and that I need to have three kids by my mid-thirties. When I get back home, I have to tell her that I'm *not* going to be doing any of those things with Malcolm. *Ever.* And she's going to kill me."

"No, she won't."

"You don't know Mama."

He laughed, causing her to do the same. Another flash from his camera captured it, but this time, she didn't mind so much.

"For instance," she added, "if she knew I was running around with you all, she'd go loco. I should act my age, she'd say. I should grow up. But what if this is how I am? What if I'm comfortable staying single and independent?"

"I think you already know the answer." Flash—another picture. "I think we all do, but it takes us a while to admit it."

She looked away from Eddie's next picture, feeling too exposed. She didn't usually spill like this to anyone but Lucy. Certainly not with other men. Even Malcolm had posted limits on what kind of conversations they had.

Carmen had grown to resent that, too.

Eddie stopped with the pictures. "Hey."

When she didn't answer, he moved closer, taking her glass and putting it on the table, then skimming a finger over her cheek. She trembled, coming alive at the touch.

"What if," she whispered, "I give in to the pressure and accept that I'm supposed to be a married thirty-year-old?"

"Don't do it."

"Sure." Her laugh was hardly happy. "I'll just ignore all the signs and pretend I'm forever twenty. Will that work instead?"

Without answering—not with words, anyway—he stroked her cheek, as if appreciating the structure of her face. Then he caressed down to her neck, the tender skin, the veins that she knew were getting more visible by the year.

But when he sketched back up to her jaw, when he eased back her hair, she saw something marvelous in his gaze: a fervent admiration. It went beyond her appearance into what he might have seen *in* her, even from the first second they'd met.

Something *she* hadn't even seen yet.

She ached between her legs—twisty and pained, but in a good, swelling way.

"You have no idea what you do to a man," he said, so close that she could breathe him in. "Do you?"

"Eddie..." She wanted to argue, but why? She'd been doing it her whole life, doubting herself and staying with Malcolm out of pure habit and duty.

Now, with a man looking at her with such brutal yearning, she didn't have the will to argue.

Carmen's pulse stomped throughout her body, a red light blinding her defenses. *How far do you want this to go?* it said in some kind of code. *How intense?*

Just intense enough to allow her to leave when she was satiated, she thought.

Her lips tingled in remembrance of their kiss in the motel. Only a kiss, and it had lured her here, where she had something to prove to herself—a bravery she needed to discover before she got back home.

And maybe she should start now.

She reached behind her neck, where her bathing-suit top was tied. As she eased down the material, her breasts puckered in the air, in the open where any of the kids could see them.

When he glanced down at her, she held her breath. Was he used to twenty-one-year-old breasts that hadn't even started the swan-dive sag? Breasts like Trudy's?

Latent suspicion traced through her. Before today, she hadn't allowed herself to even think he'd been with any of the girls. He hadn't seemed interested.

So why now?

"Perfect," he said, looking back into her eyes. "You're so perfect, Carmen."

He guided her back into the kitchen, where they found some shelter behind a bank of cupboards. Hidden, he traced her nipple, stimulating her. And when he leaned down to kiss it, she closed her eyes, thinking she might scream.

The water slapped against the houseboat, sounding louder than it had earlier. It reminded her that the rest of the group was around, liable to walk in at any time.

But when Eddie eased a hand over her ribs, she didn't care much. She only pressed against his mouth as he took her breast in, sucking her and swirling his tongue.

Opening her eyes, she looked down at him, running her hand through his carefree hair as he laved her.

Then he slid up her body, his mouth catching hers in a kiss—wet, ferocious and starving.

They melted together, tongues tangling as she stumbled back, unbalanced. Her body flamed, her nipples brushing his chest, her breasts flattening against him when she hit the counter and he cushioned the back of her with his arms.

He came up for air, their mouths still brushing.

"How long can you stay with me?" he asked.

"I…" She tried to think straight, but the humidity of their bodies was clouding everything. "Lucy… She's waiting back onshore."

"With her own guy." Eddie nipped at Carmen's lower lip, then let it slide out of his mouth in an endless suck.

Carmen pressed into him, feeling his erection. The ridge of it nudged her, stimulating her clit.

"But I'm with Lucy," she said, the protest weak.

He pulled back, framing her shoulders with his hands, his fingers coasting down her arms then stroking her breasts.

She'd almost forgotten about her state of dress. Revealed, when he'd revealed nothing to her.

But wasn't that supposed to be the appeal? Wasn't that what she'd told Lucy about strangers on that first day? It wasn't his fault that she'd made the mistake of talking too much.

It's just that… Well, it would be nice to hear a man speak the truth for once. Malcolm hadn't done much of that, and she seemed to be getting a repeat performance from Eddie.

The moment gone, she glanced away from him and tied her bathing suit back in place. She didn't know what to say now, because he had to be disappointed.

Then, as if on cue, she heard a yell from outside, and through the window, she saw that the kid who Lucy thought looked like Roy Rogers—Shawn was his name—had caught a fish. He was holding it up like a trophy on a line, high-fiving the other kids.

When her phone rang, she dived for it, not looking at Eddie. Unable to.

She felt his frustration though. It tweaked the hairs on the back of her neck as she grasped her cell.

But what did she owe him?

Stranger encounters were great because you ended up not owing them a darn thing, right?

"Luce?" she asked after checking the ID and answering, hoping that nothing was wrong and that this was just a general check-in.

"Hey, Carm."

Her friend paused, and Carmen sensed trouble.

"Don't panic," Lucy said, "but I'm not in Lake Havisu anymore."

AS LUCY MADE her announcement, she watched the cowboy while he chatted with a Native American man behind the counter of his Oatman jewelry shop. They were in a small, rough-wooded boutique, with necklaces, rings and bracelets poised for sale on tree branches, behind glass display cases and against black velvet posted on the walls.

The stranger glanced at her from under the shade of his hat while the owner, Mr. Graham, reached under his display case to extract a piece. She smiled at the cowboy, indicating that all was well, and he winked.

Lucy's stomach flip-flopped. Boy, she'd really done it this time.

She prepared for Carmen's shock and it wasn't far behind.

"What!" her friend said on the other end of the line.

Holding the phone away from her ear, Lucy made an "oh, my" face to the cowboy, then put the cell back in place again.

"I told you not to panic," she said. "It's no big thing."

"No big thing? Where are you? And why are you there instead of here?"

"Because this is the real Lucy." Seemed enough of a sufficient explanation. "I'm the girl who isn't tied to a reason."

Carmen went silent, and Lucy wondered if her friend's reaction had anything to do with how *she* was wishing she didn't have any kind of timetable or expectations to meet, either. Even if her carefree friend talked the talk, she had a lot to account for with her family.

"I'm going to keep in touch, Carm, just like I promised," Lucy said, turning away from the cowboy and facing a wall of draped silver belts studded with stones. "You've got the cowboy's license number, but nothing bad is going to happen, so you won't need it. Truly."

"You can't make those kinds of vows," Carmen said, hardly assuaged. "And 'keep in touch'? You're going to be back here tomorrow, right?"

"Tomorrow night. Of course."

"Okay."

But one of those rebellious urges had ripped through Lucy again—the same kind that had caused her to take that first impulsive turn out of Peggy Sue's and onto the highway. She didn't want to think about tomorrow, even though she wanted Carmen to be reassured.

"You still haven't told me where you are," Carmen said.

"Close by."

"Lucy!"

"Carm." She pointed a finger in the air, as if her friend would be able to see how strongly she felt about keeping her location mum. But how could she clearly explain that secrecy was part of her newfound freedom?

Revealing her whereabouts would only mean that she hadn't really escaped from the empty spaces she'd seen stretching before her in life. If Lucy didn't make a change, she would end up alone in her bed at night, in a darkness that allowed her to think too much. And she didn't like how that darkness isolated her, bringing every suspicion that she would end up alone true.

She kept her finger up, as if it supported her last-ditch attempt to avoid becoming her worst fears.

"I'll surprise you with the location tomorrow," she said. "But for now, just trust me."

She could almost see Carmen's hackles rise over the phone line. Wrong thing to request of a woman who had such Malcolm issues, but throughout their friendship, Lucy believed she'd earned this one thing.

"Okay?" Lucy repeated.

"I've got a bad feeling about this."

"And that makes it all the sweeter. You good on your end?"

"Yes, but—"

"Then go and be wild and free, babe. I'll see you soon."

As they signed off, Carmen still didn't sound happy, but Lucy knew her friend would come around. She had to stop worrying so much. Lucy knew from experience what a drag it was.

She'd already checked in with her brother, taking care not to tell him the details of who she was with—let him still think she was a virgin, for heaven's sake. Besides, she would also call her parents sometime tonight to say she loved them, just as she always did. She was definitely covered.

But now it was all about her stranger.

Going to the counter to nestle by his side, she noticed that he was holding a bamboo-link choker with a turquoise pendant as a centerpiece. She'd been admiring it earlier.

"Maybe you could put that on and I'll inspect you with devoted admiration," Mr. Graham said, crinkles framing his brown eyes. His face was a map of laugh lines, his skin leathery under his feather-accented cowboy hat.

Her stranger glanced up from the jewelry. "I'll give her all the admiration she needs."

He broke into an amiable grin, and the shopkeeper waggled his eyebrows.

Lucy's pulse fluttered. Her cowboy sounded kind of jealous, or at least possessive. She shouldn't have wanted that, but it felt nice anyway.

"I'd like the choker though," she said, reaching for her wallet. "How much?"

Before Mr. Graham could talk, the cowboy put his hands on her shoulders and turned her away from him. "I've already taken care of it."

"You bought it?"

The owner's laugh was tobacco gritted. "He's giving you a gift, sweetheart. Accept it gracefully."

The cowboy lifted her hair, pushing its thickness to the side, and then slid the jewelry around her throat. She reached up to feel the turquoise, overwhelmed by this token. He didn't have to do this. It wasn't a part of what she'd imagined.

Abruptly, she realized that she'd structured her fantasy, too. And that meant she was the same old Lucy, caught in a never-ending cycle.

Rebelling again, she let go of all expectation.

"Thank you," she said over her shoulder as he spread her hair out.

She caught the look on his face, and it sent a wash of lust through her. Enraptured? Was that what he was?

By her? Lucy Christie?

She caught herself middoubt. This was something else she would have to change—not believing that she was worth it, that a man would want to stick around for her even if she didn't push him to. She'd spent so much time being rejected that she'd come to believe the worst.

But that didn't make sense with this cowboy, who was looking at her as if she was the be-all and end-all.

When Mr. Graham cleared his throat to cut through the intimacy, she dragged her gaze away, blushing.

"You're welcome," she heard the cowboy say softly.

There was a trace of…something…in his tone. An undercurrent that she couldn't comprehend.

Avoiding it, she bought some silver feather earrings for Carmen, then said goodbye to the shopkeeper, exiting into the dusty street. But Lucy could barely put one foot in front of the other. She was that weak-kneed.

They walked past the hitching posts in front of other shops, past the parked cars, past the burros that were said to be wild descendants of the ones the miners had brought here. Their sole purpose was to wander around, looking for food from tourists, then return to the hills when the town shut down for the day.

"You didn't have to do that, you know," Lucy said, touching the choker. "But thank you again."

"You have this and I have your panties. *And* I have ulterior motives."

She raised an eyebrow at him.

He tipped up his hat in a manner that was too cocky to be completely "aw shucks."

"I want to see you in nothing else but that jewelry," he said.

She almost went liquid then and there.

Doing her best to volley back, she said, "I noticed that you picked a stone that clashed with my red-and-white top, the better to get the clothing off me. Clever of you, Mr. Cowboy. Very clever."

They came to the adobe-faced Oatman Hotel, where they'd already checked in. They'd thought to rent the Gable-Lombard room for the night, but more than anything, it was a display piece that allowed tourists to take a gander, with mementos and a window in the door. The viewing square had a shade, of course, but Lucy hadn't liked the idea of disturbing what seemed like a tribute to past glory.

So they'd checked into a room on the opposite side and down the hall. No one else seemed to be staying on the premises though, and the bare halls almost sang of ghosts.

"Hungry?" the cowboy asked as they passed the steps leading to the rooms and headed for the restaurant/bar instead.

"I could stand a bite." It was going to be a long night, and the cheese and fruit from this afternoon wasn't going to hold.

As they sat down at a time-scarred table, she took in the clutter of the Old West room. Dollars decorated the walls, and the barmaid told them that miners used to pin their bills there before going back to work, just so they'd have enough drinking money when they returned to town. Antique tin signs, like a round red Coca-Cola ad, and paraphernalia, like washboards and small brooms, provided a warm ambience in spite of the gray-planked walls.

After they ordered drinks—bottled beer for him, soda for her—they listened to the crowd around them, the tourists on their way to other destinations tonight.

Lucy smiled. She had nowhere to be.

Yet…for a moment, it left her floundering.

Then she grabbed back onto where she was, who she was with. A cowboy, minding his manners by taking off his hat and hanging it on the back of a chair, his hair dark, his eyes pale and ice-hot.

He saw her watching him and, before she could even remember to breathe again, he'd leaned over, his expression pulse-stutteringly serious as he caressed her cheek.

He didn't say it, but she knew what he was no doubt asking again.

Who are you?

She had no answers. Not anymore.

9

WHEN DAWN TILTED through the unshaded hotel window, illuminating a room that looked as if a miner might be right at home in it, Joshua was already awake.

He had liked the idea of rising and shining to a bare view of the morning. But more importantly, the anticipation of seeing the sunrise cover the woman beside him in bed excited his senses even more.

In fact, he'd been so stimulated that he hadn't actually ever *gone* to sleep. Having sex most of the night could've had something to do with keeping him up though.

And in more ways than one.

Sitting up in the rickety old bed, Joshua ran a hand over his face, then ruffled his hair. The brunette still lay sleeping, her dark locks splayed over the pillow, her hand resting next to a face that seemed almost angelic in repose.

But, farther down, sheets gathered just below her hipbones, and that tempered some of her innocence. There was just something about naked breasts tipped by dark pink nipples that signified temptation to a man who was all too willing to sin.

Joshua's skin tingled. He'd tasted those breasts last night, tasted every other pink part of her over and over again until she had fallen into an exhausted slumber.

From that point on, Joshua had mostly lain awake, hearing the eerie bray of a burro that was still wandering the street. His imagination had taken it from there, conjuring all the ghosts that were supposed to haunt this old hotel.

Lonely, he had thought as he watched his lover while sleep made her chest gently rise and fall.

He had felt lonelier than he could've ever imagined, and he thought he knew why now.

This woman reminded him of home because he'd always wanted what had lived there: love. And throughout his life, as he'd taken all the women, all the possible affection, for granted, he'd never dwelled on the emotion. Not until his dad had lost his mom and Joshua had lost the land.

Now he wanted it all—the property *and* the feelings. The innocence of accepting someone who fit him perfectly, even if the connection was chemical and unspoken right now.

Yet it could be more, Joshua thought, finally wishing to accept it. Much more.

As if sensing the light creeping through the window, his no-name brunette stirred, stretching her arms and drawing in a long breath. Then she opened her eyes, smiling lazily in the pale morning.

His heart clutched, emphasizing how empty it'd been.

They didn't say anything at first, just got used to each other all over again. But maybe there wasn't anything left to talk about since she hadn't allowed either of them to verbally provide anything of substance.

She reached for the half-full glass of wine that rested on the wobbly wooden nightstand. After sipping from it, she put it back down and reclined.

"Morning breath," she mumbled. "Who needs it?"

Following suit, he scooped his bottle of beer from the floor and took a swig. They'd brought up some drinks from the bar before it'd closed last night.

He gave her a knowing grin.

They both laughed softly. It was too quiet, even if they suspected that no one else was in the hotel…or in town, for that matter. They weren't even sure if there was a caretaker around.

She stretched again, as if her body needed to work out the positions he'd put her through last night.

"Were you watching me because I snore?" she asked. "Please tell me I don't."

"You don't."

"Thank God."

He wondered how many men she'd asked the same question. A spike of envy thrust at him, but he didn't know why. It couldn't be important, even if he had become enamored of this woman's spirit, the vitality she had that he sorely required himself.

Setting his beer back on the floor, he said, "I was only looking you over, trying to get more hints about you."

Her gaze filled with that odd expression he'd noticed before. "And what did you find out?"

"Nothing. Just that you don't move around much during slumber time. See how the sheets around you are still nice and neat while on my side of the bed…?"

He gestured to how the linen tangled with his legs.

"You're restless." She tugged at the sheets covering his nethers. "That's what sleep says about *you.* I seem to be a much calmer napper."

"Great. Now I know more about you when you're sleeping than when you're awake." He yanked his section of the sheet away from her grasp and secured it over his groin. "I'm striking gold by the minute."

There was that look again: definitely something like...

Wariness.

That was it. A caution that went beyond the pseudodanger of their games.

Games she insisted on playing. Games he was ready to leave behind, except for the fact that he was pretty sure it wouldn't take her long to leave him once she'd had her fun.

Joshua fell into a reverie of what-ifs.

What would've happened between them if they'd met up before Trent had screwed Joshua over? Would she have perceived him to be more of a man, one with decent qualities that hadn't been shadowed by crisis?

More to the point, would it have been harder for her to define him as this nobody who was currently servicing her?

Frustration overcame him. He had a name, an identity, a family and friends. He even had a chance to right the wrongs done to his kin and, damn it all, he wanted her to know that he existed as more than a nonentity.

His body went taut, and she must've predicted that the change could only mean a serious attempt at conversation.

Rolling out of bed, she said, "Think I'll hit the shower early."

He thought of the simple, shared facilities down the hall. Not very romantic in there, not even as roomy as his truck.

"Why the hurry?" he asked. "No one else is around this place. It's not as if you'll have to beat the crowd." He laid back down. "Unless you want to get on the road and go back to Carmen."

"She'll still be out on the houseboat..."

The brunette seemed tempted to add more, yet she didn't.

Instead, she assumed a neutral expression, donned a nightdress from her belongings and grabbed a beauty bag before opening the door.

"See you in a few," she said, sending him a promising smile as she left.

And...once again, he found himself alone with the ghosts and the dawn.

Damn it, what should he make of her?

He must've drifted off under the weight of the question because, before he knew it, she was back, water still dewing her shoulders and curling her dark hair.

Nature called, so he got up to put on his jeans, kissed her wet shoulder, then ambled down the hall to brush his teeth and grab a quick shower.

When he got back, she was facing the window, running a comb through her damp hair.

Buck naked.

He closed the door behind him, his cock showing interest by going board stiff.

"Tease," he said.

"Sucker," she said right back, turning around to face him.

As orange and pink shimmered through the window, his gaze traveled up her long legs, then the dark thatch of hair that covered her sex. He continued upward, over her slender waist, her breasts...

Sweet heaven, she was wearing the choker he'd purchased for her yesterday.

And that was all.

Now his penis was fully erect, clamoring to be inside her, where he knew she would feel tight and soft, drenched for him.

"Since we woke up so early," she said, tossing her comb into her bag on the floor, "I figured we could have one for the road."

"Then get over here before the burros see you through the window."

She sauntered over to him, coming to stand inches away, where he could feel the heat of her skin, even from a near distance. It flared into him, pumping up his temperature, his pulse.

He couldn't help leaning in closer, just to smell her, to taunt her. His cock brushed her pubic hair, inflaming him further.

She sucked in a breath, then cupped his penis, parting her legs so she could guide his tip through her damp folds.

Groaning, he braced his hands on her shoulders. His nerve endings screamed and, instinctively, he nudged the opening of her sex with his arousal, seeking entrance.

"Wait," she said.

Condom. *Damn* it.

He cursed some more while securing one, sheathing himself and then turning back to her, grabbing her hips in one fluid movement while he sat on the bed. Without further preamble, he brought her onto his lap, impaling her, and she threw back her head, letting out a surprised, ecstatic cry.

He wanted to say her name, but he couldn't. It just stuck in his throat until she pushed him back onto the mattress, where the pressure of an exclamation came out in a fierce grunt.

She rode him, hard and rough, working him until steam gathered in his belly, his cock. On and on until he couldn't take any more, past that point, beyond anything he'd ever endured.

With a dissipating crash, he came, his skin vulnerable with sensation, his emotions built to a point where he couldn't contain them.

"What're you doing to me?" he grated, body on fire.

She smiled cryptically, but before she could give him

another one of her flip answers, he maneuvered himself so that he was on top of her, hovering, seething.

Even in his raw fury, he could see that she was on the edge of a climax. Cruelly, he withheld it from her.

Two could play this game.

He used his penis—erect even now—to tease her sex. She wiggled beneath him, biting her lip, but the gleam in her eyes told him she was still playing.

"How far are you going to take this?" he asked. "How far should *I* go?"

He pressed his tip against her clit, and she winced.

"Come on, cowboy," she whispered, her tone jagged.

He came close to telling her his name, claiming her in some odd way, but he wanted her to work for it now, just as he had worked so hard for her.

And that's exactly what he had been doing, he realized. Working himself around from being the bitter man who had first hit the road to being someone who sought more value than that.

He was going to prove his worth, too…

Separating her legs, he went down on her, brutally loving her with his mouth, his tongue, manipulating her clit until she pulled at his hair and rocked against him.

When she yelled out her orgasm, it was a wordless mangle, and he wondered if she regretted not knowing his name then.

As she caught her breath, loosening her nailed hold on his shoulders, morning grew stronger and his blood slowed to a lurching crawl. He slid up her body, sweat sticking them together in a physical bond—the only one they had.

He rolled over and took her with him, chest to chest, skin to skin. She accepted his embrace, wrapping her arms around him. But he knew this kind of intimacy might end up chasing her away as soon as she had time to realize what she was doing, and that was the last thing he wanted.

So he took a chance.

"And to think," he said, "we've got all day for more, if you want."

She stiffened, but only for a moment before she went pliant, burrowing her face into his neck.

"I do want," she said, before sighing against him.

And that was good enough for now.

CARMEN HADN'T SLEPT well last night on the houseboat, even in the bed that she'd been given.

She'd shared it with Sarah, the marine biology student, and the rest of the bunch had used everything from the second bedroom to the main room's floor.

That's where Eddie had slumbered, for all Carmen knew, because after their disagreement and then Lucy's phone call, she'd been too wired to even think of getting it on with the guy she'd been pursuing.

If only she'd just stuck with Lucy's original travel plans.

She got out of bed while fingers of orange and red tickled the sky, then discovered Richie brewing coffee in the kitchen. She glanced at the sleeping bodies on the floor, trying to recognize Eddie, but both forms had the blankets pulled over their heads, as if to keep out Richie's kitchen puttering.

Was one of them Eddie?

Or was he in that second bedroom with Trudy?

No, she wouldn't make a drama out of this, so she went to the deck, where Richie soon joined her with coffee. They talked softly about his engineering classes as well as some Web sites they both frequented.

But every time she broached the subject of Eddie, Richie clammed up.

Were these people some kind of Kool-Aid cult following a leader who told them to keep quiet as he lured Carmen into his clutches?

She had to laugh at herself. Overreact much?

Out of the sheer need to get out of her funk, Carmen shed her sarong cover-up and dived into the water, surfacing and heaving in air.

Cold!

Richie did the same, and they ended up quietly splashing around like kids before climbing back up the deck ladder and swaddling themselves in towels.

Just as the others were starting to mill around, she got a call on her cell. Lucy.

"Morning, sunshine," Carmen said.

"Morning. Whatcha up to?"

She filled Lucy in. "Richie says we're supposed to stop by the dock when late afternoon comes around. Then I think Eddie's going to take his pictorial side trip on the Route while the others go out on the lake again."

And, Carmen thought, the change in routine would pretty much spell the end of her Eddie time.

She told herself that, with the way things were going, a parting was cool with her. Besides, she couldn't wait to see Lucy again and hear about her escapade.

Yet the sentiments rang hollow.

"When are you heading back?" Carmen asked.

"Well, I..." Lucy started. "Um..."

Trepidation sneaked up on her. "You I...er...um what?"

"I'm kind of on the Route myself."

Carmen almost dropped the phone, and Richie widened his eyes at her obvious shock.

"Where on the Route?" She hushed down, mindful that others still might be sleeping. "Oh, man, Lucy…"

"I swear, Carmen, this is it. I'll be back tomorrow." She paused, as if that cowboy were right next to her and she was giving him one of her patented Cute Lucy Grins. "I *swear.*"

Carmen took a breath then let it out slowly. She had created this horny monster, so she wouldn't chastise. She wouldn't fuss, either. That would make her too much like Mama, and Carmen stiffened at the notion.

Was it because she couldn't ever picture herself with her mother's life? Mama was a woman who seemed to control everyone now because Carmen suspected she didn't have many choices herself at this point. Not that Mama appeared to be unhappy, but there were times when she saw something in the older woman's eyes that looked like faded dreams.

Carmen put a defensive hand on her hip. "You're not telling me where you are?"

"You'll know once I bring you back souvenirs."

Lucy was pulling the charm act on her now, and Carmen sighed.

"Hey," her friend said, "I'm still safe, and I'm still very happy."

What, were Lucy and her fling headed toward Vegas to get hitched or something? In spite of Lucy's organizational passions, she had always been ready to go a little wild. It's just that she'd had too much of a straitlaced upbringing to do it quickly. Shedding old ways took time.

"How's Eddie?" her friend asked.

Ignoring the change of subject, Carmen said, "Fine. Spectacular. But why can't you and your cowboy just do your thing back here?"

"All's cool. Believe me." Someone—the cowboy, Carmen would bet—said something, and Lucy answered. Then she was back on the phone. "Gotta go. Love ya, Carm!"

"Lu—"

But the line was already dead.

Carmen thought about redialing, but that would make her Mama. Did she have reason to be amping out like this or was she just overreacting again?

A voice spoke from behind her. "Another call?"

It was Eddie. Carmen turned around to find him dressed in new jeans and a blue T-shirt, his sandy hair wet and in disarray. In spite of all her misgivings, her heart clenched at the sight. So damn cute.

"Lucy's still off and running," she said.

Richie sneaked away, into the main cabin, and Eddie took his place on the lounge chair across from her. The morning air was fresh, and the water glistened, as if waking itself up.

"You're worried," he said.

"Slightly. I know Lucy can handle herself, but… Heck, it's her first time doing something like this."

Eddie chuckled, taking a drink from the coffee he was holding.

"What's so funny?" she asked.

He shrugged. "I guess when I first saw you sitting in that diner, with your hair—" he motioned toward his head, imitating a follicle explosion "—and that punk tank top…"

"You thought I was straight out of a mosh pit."

"You threw your head back when you laughed, like you didn't care about anything. I really liked that. Liked it a lot."

Carmen realized that she'd never been that garage-band-shirt-wearing girl at all. She had dressed that way forever, but she'd had Malcolm to keep her mentally grounded. She'd had Lucy, too, back when her friend had possessed a level head.

Before the birth of Sexzilla.

And...well, she guessed that she'd also had herself to monitor those hedonistic urges all the other kids around her had given in to.

She'd had herself all along and she hadn't even known it.

The realization shocked her, but it comforted her, too. She had herself. *Her* choices, not her family's.

"But after getting to know you a little," Eddie added, "I get it. You're the nurturing type, even if you don't want to commit to anyone right now."

She couldn't say anything, not when a stranger seemed to know her better than she had ever known herself. Or maybe it'd just taken her a long time to recognize that she was a mother hen.

God, but that's not what she wanted, either. Marriage, kids, all the rest...

A future of that gave her the hives.

"I'm not my mom," Carmen said, standing up.

"Who says you have to be?"

She wanted to leave this conversation, but where else would she go on this boat? It was only so big and Eddie would catch up sometime. And even if he might not ever continue their discussion, she would know it had gone unresolved.

It unnerved her that he guessed so darn much about her.

"Listen," Eddie said, calmly looking up at Carmen, his forearms on his thighs as he held his mug. "If you want me to hire a P.I., I can. For Lucy. If you're that worried."

"No, that's definitely going too far." She frowned. "P.I.'s aren't cheap, either."

"Sometimes they're a good investment."

Another vague statement hooking her in to wondering even more about him.

Her frustration with him came to a boil. "What do you mean by that, Eddie? How do you have enough money to be throwing it around on houseboats and P.I.'s? And what's with you hanging around these kids you seem to have nothing in common with? What's going on?"

Silently, he rose to a stand, his jaw tight. "I can take you to the docks, Carmen, and if you need more help, all you have to do is ask. Other than that…I'm sorry."

Her mouth opened, ready to fire off more questions at him. But something told her it would only force him back, away from her.

And that's not what she longed for. She wanted…

Well, it had turned out *not* to be sex. At least not right now.

So what was it?

In the back of her mind, the answer took form, just as if she had been staring at a Rorschach test and the picture suddenly made some sense.

It wasn't just his youth and the buried longings that came with it. There was another quality about Eddie Kilpatrick that drew her. The way he listened. The way he seemed to understand Carmen without her having to explain her opinions or feel guilty about them.

More importantly, she wanted the option of showing herself that she could bring someone so patently wrong for her home. That she had made her own choice in who she wished to be with for the time being.

She looked at Eddie straight on. "You're going on the road today?"

"I planned to."

Ask him, Carmen. Pursue what you *want.*

She gathered her guts and went for it. "See, Lucy has the keys to our car, and I know she's somewhere not too far away. I wonder if looking at the places she was interested in before she took off might—"

"Then let's get going," Eddie said, not requiring any further explanation.

Which made perfect sense.

SHE WOULD NEVER have this chance again, Lucy thought. So why not go for it all?

When the cowboy had suggested that they spend the day at Grand Canyon Caverns, a Route 66 institution located only a couple of hours away, she'd agreed, her body pressed against his after she'd experienced the best sex ever.

Being in such a position, how could she possibly say no?

Okay, her mind had been muddled, but she didn't regret it.

The only thing that allowed Lucy to take one more day away from Havisu was that Carmen was with Eddie, having her own good times. Besides, Lucy would be back soon; this was only a side trip. A fling that had almost run its course.

So she had hopped into the stranger's truck to head east with him.

Things had gone just as well as they had in Oatman. They'd laughed, relaxed, listened to a seventies rock station that was barely more music then static.

And then he had gotten a phone call.

He had taken only one glimpse at his cell before muttering that he had to pick up, then pulled off the road and into a rusted, closed gas station.

As she waited in the truck, she watched the cowboy, his broad back turned to her, the phone to his ear. Behind him, an old Texaco sign lay on its side, as if it'd been pushed over and never gotten back up. Faded red gasoline pumps waited for one last customer, seeming forlorn at the lack of traffic.

Suddenly, the cowboy took off his hat and swung it around at whatever news he'd just gotten. Laughing, he hunkered down to his haunches, where he continued talking, but with more animation this time.

More than what she'd ever seen from him.

Lucy realized that she was *this* close to his personal life. Too close.

Soon, he ended the call and headed back toward the truck. His hat was back on where it normally was—guarding his gaze as it cast shade over his face, his pale eyes glowing under the brim.

Dust kicked around his boots as he ambled closer. A cloud rolled over the sun, stealing some light.

All the while, her heart warmed in her chest, and she pressed her hand to it.

Opening the door, he started to tell her something, just barely able to contain his joy. But then he held up his hands, cutting himself off.

"What—" she began to ask. She'd been focusing too hard on making herself go cold again, and he'd caught her off guard.

But it wasn't working, the cold-heart thing. And, dang it, she really did want to know *one* thing about him. Just one.

What would be the harm, if their time was ending soon anyway?

She found herself trying again. "What was that all about?"

He paused, as if weighing whether she truly wanted to hear it or not. Then, without warning, he sprang into the truck and scooped her into his arms, laying the kiss of all kisses on her.

Dizzy...his lips on hers, his arms enveloping her...the scent of him becoming a part of her...

Then he cupped her face between his hands, his eyes shining. Her lips throbbed, tingled, craved more.

"Oil." He laughed, and it sounded like some kind of release. "It looks like there could be oil on my land. I need to get back now, to be there so I can see to the details."

He broke into bigger laughter—crazy, overjoyed, complete laughter that invited her to join in.

She did. "Congratulations. I...gosh."

What could she say? This was so unexpected, so...wow.

And so none of her business.

Still...oil? *Oil?*

He must've sensed that he had ignored the stranger rule with his news, because he drew away, searching her face, then stroking back her hair before letting her go altogether.

"I guess you're a rich one then," she said lightly, telling herself that his distance didn't hurt. She'd caused it, after all. "A big tycoon."

"I'm—" He cut himself off, then stared out the windshield, a smile taking over his lips. "I'm free to go home now. That's all I am."

He didn't start the car. A semitruck roared past them, shuddering their vehicle. It felt like a precursor of some sort.

And she was right.

Slowly, he took off his hat, as if to open himself, then he

looked at her. His gaze held such jarring wattage that she held her breath.

Don't feel this *free, cowboy,* she thought. *Don't say anything.*

But when he started, he couldn't seem to stop, no matter how hard she tried not to listen.

"I live in Fielding, Texas," he said. "A little town in the east. Grew up on a horse-breeding farm, where we had paints and palominos for sale. Acres and acres of beautiful land that had been in the family for generations. And then my dad took over, running the place for years before…"

He cleared his throat. "Understand, now, that my mom had died three years earlier, and Dad wasn't over it. I saw how it broke him, how it took the care right out of him. He didn't have the strength to be helming a business, and I should've seen it, except I was off advising other companies about how to best run their own holdings. Then Dad died, and my sisters asked me to come home. I found out just what he'd done to the ranch then, just what he'd left us with."

She was hearing it all, drinking up every sentence as if she couldn't get enough.

"We had a family friend," he continued, "a neighbor who said he would do anything to help us avoid bank foreclosure. Timothy Trent said he'd buy most of our property and hold it, just until we could afford to purchase it back from him. That's what he said, at least. But he betrayed my family."

He paused, a dark fire in his eyes. "The irony is that my associate who's doing the testing just found documentation that, unbeknownst to anyone else in the family, my father had quietly done his own surveys on some of our land, mostly the parts that my neighbor stole, but he never got to all of our holdings. According to the old work, what Timothy Trent has is bone dry."

The fire in his eyes banked, and he leaned back against his seat with a wry grin. "Come to find out, too, that the community—Fielding and the ranch's business associates—got wind of what Trent did and they've shut him out of everything. That means when I get back, I can drive him to the brink, and just before he falls over it, I'll give him back his original money. I'll get back what's ours and no more. That's all I want. His reputation is going to take care of the rest."

She'd never seen the cowboy so relaxed, as if weights had been on his shoulders and this news had removed them. She wanted to touch one of those shoulders—do something—just to see if there was any darkness remaining.

Any fantasy.

But she couldn't. She was already in too deep.

"You don't have to tell me any more," she said.

"Why? Because you have a fantasy?" The cowboy shook his head, and it was obvious that the oil news had done something else to him, given him a burning energy. "We know each other's bodies better than anyone else on this earth, I'll wager, but we don't know dip about anything else."

"That's by design."

"A bad one."

He fully turned to her, and she defensively angled back toward the door. Noting her movement, he tensed, the veins in his neck coming to pulse to the surface of his skin.

"So send me to hell for wanting to know *your* goddamn story," he said. "Is that such a terrible thing?"

Yes, she thought. *Because as soon as I start the whole clingy-Lucy thing, you'll be out of here, and I can't take that anymore.*

She turned front and center, clasping her hands in her

skirted lap. She was trembling and it was the only way she could hide it. "Just drive."

It was as if she'd stunned him. She could feel his shock in the renewed distance between them, even from his side of the cab.

Finally, he put his hat back on, but he didn't start the engine. Not yet.

"I left home because I was sorely tempted to kill the man who wronged us," he said instead. "No exaggeration there, either. And before I lost control of myself, my two sisters packed me onto the road, where I could cool off. And then I met you, this brunette in a diner who looked as sweet as springtime. You made me forget for a while."

"Stop." She couldn't know that he'd gotten attached in any way. It would be the beginning of the end, and she didn't have the strength to endure yet one more rejection, one more slap to the self-esteem she'd just built up.

"What do you want from me?" He sounded angry. "Am I humanizing myself too much? Or do you want the badass cowboy to stick around? I ran away so I wouldn't be that brute whose fingers almost wrapped around another guy's neck and squeezed the air right out of him."

She shook her head in total denial.

"But," he continued, "maybe that's what you need. That dangerous stranger."

Heat gripped her throat. She didn't know why. Maybe because hearing him say it made her fantasy into the same pathetic thing she had been escaping: something she couldn't let go of.

She swallowed, breathed, hoped she wouldn't cry. What if the only way she could be her real self *was* to be with a stranger?

What if she would never again feel the way she had during the past couple of days?

She finally tried to talk and, even though it came out as more of a choke, it echoed.

"Don't take it all away from me," she said.

"Take what..."

He trailed off, as if knowing she was emotionally flailing. Yet he didn't say a word, as if only now realizing that he had much more on his hands than just a sex-starved woman.

But when he started the engine, he didn't make a U-turn. No, he drove straight ahead, toward their intended destination, as if he accepted her wishes for the time being.

She wondered how long that would last now that their facades had been cracked.

How long it would take for him to break her even more.

10

By the time they got to Grand Canyon Caverns, a pall of clouds had gathered across the sky.

After parking the truck, Joshua took one look out the windshield and predicted a fallout day. And he wasn't just talking about the sulfur lining the air to indicate rain. *Something* was about to come down.

Something more than the taut near-discussion he'd already had with the brunette.

Things had been quiet in the truck since he'd gotten that phone call from his college friend—the geologist—who was looking into the oil seeps.

Come on home, he'd said. *I'm about to find out just how much you've got going for you on this land, Josh.*

It looked as if it might be a smaller oil field, his friend had said, but Joshua wasn't greedy. He only wanted to preserve his family heritage by claiming what Timothy Trent had taken. And since Joshua's surveyor was a friend, they had agreed to keep news of the find quiet for now, while Joshua borrowed against his future with more college friends he trusted, private lenders who would stand to profit from a strike and hopefully give him enough money to maneuver with Trent. His geology friend would be well compensated for his discretion, too.

Was it playing fast and loose? Yes, but it was no less than Trent, himself, had done with the Grays. Unless his neighbor took great steps to mend fences, he was also going to find himself with no one willing to do business.

But Joshua should get back home now, even though he could do some preliminary work from the road. He had a lot to attend to, starting with consulting an oil and gas contract attorney who'd been referred by the geologist.

Yup, he would start a marathon drive back home early tomorrow morning, barging straight through the nights and stopping at his lawyer's before he got to Fielding.

That left just one more day with the brunette.

Only one.

He watched her get out of the truck and wander over to a rest area where a T. rex replica bared its teeth at arriving tourists. Even though she had a destination, it still looked as though she was aimless.

Don't take it all away from me, she'd said back on the road.

It had been his first deep glimpse beyond the sexy nympho and into an actual person—one he found himself wanting to explore more each and every passing day.

With a last glance at the looming clouds, he grabbed a long-sleeved denim shirt from his duffel bag behind the seat, then alighted from the truck and followed her to the dinosaur.

Meanwhile, he wondered how many times he'd told himself to be careful around her. She had been only a temporary anchor, and now that he had a real, almost complete home to return to—not a substitute who had assuaged him in the interim—it was supposed to be easy to let her go.

Supposed to be.

Coming up behind her, he refrained from touching her

dark, wavy hair as the wind stroked it. He told himself not to feel the soft skin of her face with a casual caress, not to *need* to feel it.

"Can you imagine," he said softly, so as not to sneak up on her, "what it might've been like in the old days, driving through what was essentially a barren place and stopping at places like this for a taste of civilization?"

She'd been rubbing her arms, and he wasn't sure if it was for warmth or peace of mind. He would guess it was both. At any rate, he took the long-sleeved shirt and draped it over her shoulders.

The contact brought her out of her reverie, and she touched the denim, as if surprised he thought enough of her to care that she might be cold.

"Thank you," she said, pushing her hands through the sleeves and pulling it around her body.

"Don't mention it." He looked up at the T. rex. A change of subject, a retreat to neutral ground. "Sixty-six was the first direct route from Chicago to L.A., and places like these caverns built corny stuff like this guy to draw business."

"He seems kind of isolated out here without any other dinosaurs on display, doesn't he?" The brunette cocked her head, considering the lone piece of kitsch. "Like he might be excited to see every single car that pulls into the parking lot?"

"Yeah. I imagine he got real lonely when Interstate 40 came around and the original Route got relegated to side roads."

The wind moaned, and he tugged his hat down lower. It'd seemed so easy to take it off earlier, when he'd bared some of his soul to her in the truck after the phone call. He'd felt so unfettered by the oil news that revealing the rest of his life had seemed natural.

But she'd rejected his personal overture—not that he should've been surprised.

A gentleman would respect her wishes to stay strangers for one more day, he told himself. What was the point in pushing things when he had to leave anyway?

A moment passed as she inspected the T. rex then crossed her arms over her chest. "When the road broke up, that's when we changed, don't you think?"

She was talking about something more than just Route 66. More than even just society at large.

"I mean," she clarified, as if getting back on firm ground, "it's like families started breaking, too. And we all became a little more cynical."

"But the road's still here." The wind tried to cuff his hat, but he held it in place until the elements backed off. "The spirit of it will never go away."

Neither of them said anything for a second, but his brain was busy enough for all the conversation in the world.

Without her having to even say a personal word, he knew that there was a sensitive woman behind the siren. That she had maybe come on this trip with her friend for a reason other than vacation.

And he wanted to know why: wanted to know what got her out of bed every day, wanted to know what might make her happy after a long day of work, what might set her mind to rest at night so she could dream uninterrupted.

Almost as if she'd sensed that this moment had gone beyond sightseeing, she flashed a subdued smile at him and started walking toward the main building, where they'd decided to take one of the forty-five-minute cavern tours.

That's all he was going to get from her: a glimpse of more

profound feeling, a hint of what the future could've held if this had been a different time or a different place.

A dead end.

Accepting that—because what other choice was there?—he arranged their tour, then put his hand on her back and guided her to an elevator with the rest of their group.

The conveyance took them down into the natural limestone dry cavern, where their tour guide gave background about their surroundings: formed in prehistoric times, then discovered by a man on his way to a poker game in 1927 when he fell into a hole and came back with friends the next day to explore with ropes and lanterns.

At one point, the guide even turned out the atmospheric lights that highlighted the artful calcium-deposit formations, just to show them what it might be like to be trapped without illumination.

True darkness fell over them, so fathomless that Joshua found himself looking inward instead of out. And when he felt the brunette grasp his hand, he even believed that he was imagining it.

But then the lights came back on and he realized that she was actually pressed against him, pulling closed the shirt he'd draped around her earlier.

When the tour moved on, she didn't let go of him. He held on tightly, making the most of what he had left with her.

When they got back up to the top, where a curio shop and restaurant awaited, the brunette squeezed his hand in some kind of thanks for holding her, then headed outside.

"You okay?" he asked, following to make sure all was well.

"Now I am." She came to lean against her side of the truck, which faced an expanse of empty parking lot. The wind fluttered the hem of his shirt against her skirted thighs. “I didn’t like that dark part too much, so this open air feels really good.”

“The darkness didn’t last that long.”

“Long enough.”

She leaned her head back against the cab and closed her eyes.

“Damn,” he said. “It really did get to you.”

She laughed, but it sounded more like an attempt to chase away her imbalance than anything.

“I always needed the night-light when I was little,” she said. “You know, because the boogeyman was under the bed or in the closet and I thought that keeping my eyes wide open—” she saucered her gaze to emphasize her comment “—would keep him away.”

“Did it?”

Her gaze returned to normal. “Yes. I had this entire routine, I guess you could call it, where I would put a chair in front of the closet door so it would make noise if the monster crept out. And I put one of my mom’s old Christmas decorations along the line of my bed. It had bells on it, so I could hear if anything disturbed them. Then I would wait there, listening for noise until I eventually fell asleep.”

Maybe it was the darkness that had brought this all out, Joshua thought, because nothing else had encouraged her to share this much before.

He paused. Yeah, it’d been the darkness, all right. Just as the darkness of his stranger act had obviously drawn her out in a more physical way with him, too.

“Those scary days are gone though,” he said. “You can sleep now, without those bells. I’ve seen evidence.”

“I suppose it’s easier with someone else around. Darkness reminds some people that we’re really alone.” She smiled self-consciously. "It would've been nice to have some kind of company back then, as well, I think. Just someone who was *there.* My parents wouldn't let me in their room, even with the boogeyman around. My brother just laughed and told me to let him sleep. They all said I was a big girl and I could take care of it myself, so…I arranged my routine to compensate. It wasn't the first routine and it sure wasn't the last, either. I also colored inside the lines with my crayons and arranged all my toys just so."

He was watching her closely, carefully, wishing there was a way for him to take her into his arms without scaring her off.

Then, as if realizing she'd said too much, the brunette spread out her hands, putting an end to the conversation. "And there you have my life story. I hate to feel like I'm by myself, cowboy."

She turned toward the truck's door and tried the handle. Surely she hadn't expected it to be unlocked, so he suspected that she was only avoiding him now.

"I hate to tell you," he said, gently taking hold of her shoulders and turning her toward him again, "but whatever fantasy you might've had about strangers is done. We stopped not knowing each other about five orgasms and three conversations ago."

"We haven't had any conversations."

"So you think."

She shook her head. "I've told you time and again that—"

"You don't want to know me, you just want to know my body. Well, mission accomplished, darlin'. Since I've got to get home now, you've earned a tidy way to cut your ties to this whole fantasy."

She clung to the shirt he'd loaned her, gripping its hemline until she held fistfuls of denim. "All good things have to come to an end."

Her forced flippancy was the last straw, and he moved closer, unwilling to allow even an inch to separate them anymore.

"It's ridiculous that we don't even call each other by our names," he said, frustration roughening his tone. "You're not a *miss* or a *darlin'* in your normal life."

"What we've been doing isn't normal."

She levered herself away from the truck, coming face-to-face with him, toe-to-toe. Excitement overtook him at being with a woman who wouldn't stand for any crap—a strong woman. One who fit against his body so perfectly, one who captured more than his libido.

"You think our association is warped?" he asked.

"It's certainly not a straight line most people would follow." She made an obvious attempt to smooth the erratic cadence of her breathing. "Why are we even arguing about this? Talking a subject to death isn't the reason you came to my room the other night. It's not why you intercepted me at Lake Havisu, either."

"How do you know why I decided to pursue you?"

Then he stopped, on the fringe of trespassing somewhere he had no business venturing again.

This morning, the word *love* had vaguely crossed his mind. But love grew in time—he knew that from seeing his parents nurture their relationship. It came with work and devotion.

The brunette was waiting for him to finish, eyes even wider, expanded by a tinge of what he'd come to define as some kind of fear. He could read at least that much about her by now.

And when her breathing picked up and she pulled his hips to hers, he knew what she was up to.

Definite avoidance. Her *routine.*

Even so, desire flamed him with one brutal burst.

"So you just want me to shut up and do you," he said, voice tight. "That's where this is going to end."

"Are you complaining?"

Her tone was almost desperate as she reached down to his crotch and touched him. He slumped toward her, looking around instinctively to see if anyone was around to see.

No one.

Bracing his hands against the truck's cab, he lost strength because all his blood was rushing to his groin, pummeling it.

"Damn..." He tried to fight, but couldn't. It was too much of a battle and maybe he should just take what he could get.

"There," she said softly, rubbing him while he got harder and harder. "Isn't this better, cowboy?"

He surged toward a full erection, hating his body's lack of control. Hating the situation he'd gotten himself into because he didn't want to get out of it.

It couldn't end this way.

It—

With all the willpower he could muster, Joshua grabbed both her wrists, not caring how blue his balls would get, not giving a fig about the pain that would no doubt be throttling him.

She looked up at him, mouth open as if to protest, but he beat her to the punch.

"It's not *cowboy,*" he said between clenched teeth. "I'm Joshua. Got it? *Joshua.*"

In her eyes, he could see something shatter.

The force of it cut him, too, because he'd taken what he wanted, giving in to his baser urges, just as he'd been tempted to do back home with Timothy Trent. Just as he'd done all his life with the women who'd come and gone.

With a heavy heart, he realized that this trip really hadn't changed him at all.

Moments too late, Lucy shut him out, turning away and asking him to open the truck door. An escape. A necessity.

And he'd done it for her, too, even as his ragged breathing told her that she had given him a carnal pain he didn't deserve.

His name kept slashing around her head, reminding her of the reason she was retreating. Why had he done it when she'd told him time and again that she didn't want to know him?

Why hadn't he listened?

They headed back toward Lake Havisu, the radio filling the terrible silence between them. But upon arriving in Kingman, he surprised her by suggesting dinner, as if to make up for taking away her confidence, her reliance on not knowing him.

Even more surprising, dinner put them back on a lighter course, as if he was attempting to lead them off a damaged, bumpy road and onto a route with a smoother surface.

"I overstepped," he said at one point as he ate an ostrich burger and she finished her salad. "And I don't want to leave on a bad note like this."

"I'm sorry I've miffed you," she said. "But you're right. This can end much better than we left it."

Relief had swamped her at that point, and when he drove them to a cute little motel, she figured that maybe things would turn out well after all.

After checking in, they parked in front of their room in a building that looked like a cross between a Southern mansion and a rancho, with Greek columns and adobe walls. Strange, but the place seemed hospitable enough, with tea in the lobby and a rose garden in the back.

Inside, the motel had basic amenities and a laundered blue bedspread on the king-size mattress. The room even smelled lavender-soap fresh, making her think that tonight might be a clean start as well as a clean end.

She sat on the bed, waiting for him to come in. He'd gone outside in the darkening night to make phone calls to his sisters, assuring them that he would be home soon.

Beforehand, he'd told her that he wasn't planning to inform his family about the oil yet—not until he had some arrangements in hand. Lucy couldn't believe it because…

Well, he'd told *her.*

But that didn't make her special, right? She'd been there when he'd gotten the phone call, and he'd been overwhelmed by the news. It'd only been a matter of convenience and that was the extent of the gesture.

That's all. No more. No big thing.

She tapped her hands on the mattress, waiting.

One last night with the cowboy, she thought.

With…Joshua.

She tried to use her escalating desire for him to block the name out, but it didn't work. Instead, every detail he'd told her about his life came flooding back, taking her under.

Fighting, she got up from the bed, undressed and wrapped a towel around her body. Maybe a bath would do them both good when J— No, when *the cowboy* got back.

And maybe the steam would fog over her brain, too.

But she couldn't shake the invasion, the breach of all the defenses she'd erected so very carefully on this trip. It had worked for a while, hadn't it? She'd been carefree and optimistic about the next two weeks, at least.

Yet the moment the cowboy had told her his name, she'd wanted more, and she shouldn't have. More would only lead to getting attached—*too* attached. She would become needy and chase him away. It always happened.

Why should this time be any different?

Second-guessing her idea for a shared bath—the towel felt too good covering her right now—she picked up her phone instead, finding that in all her drama, it'd lost juice.

Great. She plugged her charger into the bathroom outlet, then connected that to her phone, finding a few messages from Carmen.

She speed dialed her friend, knowing she would feel better once she heard Carmen's voice. Familiarity. Her best buddy was trying to shed all her inhibitions on this trip, too, and she would talk Lucy off this emotional ledge.

When the other woman answered, she sounded incredibly relieved. "Lucy! Oh my God—"

"My darn phone drained down," she answered calmly, sensing that Carmen was at a peak of worry. "That's all, Carm. I'm so sorry about being careless."

"Where *are* you?" her friend asked.

This time, instead of keeping her secret, Lucy found herself telling Carmen her location, knowing her fantasy was ending anyway.

Or maybe it already *had* ended.

Her heart sank, and she fought the weight, the threatening connection to a situation that was never meant to last.

"We're nearby," Carmen said.

"We're?"

"Me and Eddie. I got antsy about what was happening with you and he volunteered to help me cruise around, just to see if I caught you anywhere." She paused. "That sounds so freakish, but I can't help it. We're not the type of women who do these things, Luce, and I'm not sure how to go about dealing with it."

"And," Lucy added, feeling worse than ever, "I have the car keys because I thought you'd be staying on the house-boat longer."

"It's okay, you shouldn't have expected me to wig out, just like Mama would've. Because, you realize, that's who I was becoming. Mama Ferris. Not anymore though."

Eddie's voice said something in the background, and Carmen laughed softly, as if she didn't quite believe whatever he'd offered.

"You'll never be Mama," Lucy said. "Mama would've still been back at the Timberline Inn telling the desk clerk how to improve the property."

"Know what?" Carmen said. "We're off subject, Luce. You've gotten pretty good at that."

Her? "Listen to you—the girl who hasn't told me much about what's going on in her mind, either, lately."

Silence. Then, "I know."

The line went quiet until Lucy offered a laugh. Carmen followed, and the static was a little clearer between them.

But not totally, because it was about time Lucy let go of her fantasy and let Carmen in.

God, it was really over.

"My cowboy is leaving in the morning," she said, voice raw. "My schedule's clear if yours is."

His name's Joshua, she thought to herself. *Why can't you call him by his real name, even now?*

"He's...leaving?" Carmen asked tentatively, as if knowing how much it would hurt Lucy when another man ducked out of her life.

"He has to," Lucy said. "Something came up at home for him."

"Then he actually wants to stay? He wouldn't be leaving otherwise?"

A lump in her throat made it tough to talk. Right now, his leaving might not have the power to damage her. She was still in control of the situation—just looking into his eyes told her that.

And that *should've* felt so good.

"Luce," Carmen said, "what if this time, he *could* stay?"

She wouldn't even entertain the idea. From experience, she knew that crushed hope was too agonizing. "He wouldn't hang around anyway."

Once she said it, she knew it had no place in her life now.

Carmen only confirmed it. "You're sure? Because I've seen a different Lucy lately. You've been walking around with a…solidness, I suppose you'd say. And I can't tell you how beautiful it is to see."

There were tears in her friend's voice, and it was catching. Lucy rested her head against the restroom tile, needing something to help her remain standing.

"But here's the thing," she managed to say to Carmen. "He only knows *this* Lucy, the one who's on vacation. I'm pretty sure he would've been gone by now if he'd met the old, boring version."

"Okay, first of all, you've never been boring. You like your schedules? Yes. You're comfortable in a routine? Sure. But, Luce, you've always had a sparkle to you." Carmen laughed. "Do you think I would've chosen you as a partner in crime if you didn't?"

Lucy wiped a tear away, hating that this was enough to upset her.

"And second?" Carmen added. "You won't know until you try, so why don't you give this guy a chance?"

Because it's so much easier now, she thought. So much simpler to keep him as a good memory than a bad one.

She stood away from the wall, knowing she needed to stop before Carmen talked her into doing the unthinkable—introducing the cowboy to the hidden Lucy.

"Are you and Eddie checking in here tonight then?" she asked, putting an end to any temptation.

On the other end of the line, Carmen sighed, noting that, once again, the subject had been changed. Then her friend asked Eddie a question, and he seemed to give a positive answer.

"We'll aim the car for your motel," Carmen said. "We're pretty close anyway, near Seligman, since we've been checking the Route's hot spots all day for a sign of that cowboy's truck. We must've passed you at some point without knowing."

"We were at Grand Canyon Caverns, then we backtracked. Maybe we'd pulled off the road for Kingman by the time you passed us."

"Well, then it'll be bedtime when we check in, so I'll see you in the morning?"

"Late morning." Lucy knew she would need the extra time with her playmate.

Just as Carmen was going to need extra time with her own fling.

Lucy clung to the established definitions—*playmate, fling.* Still structured.

She would always be the same girl, sexed up or not.

The sound of the front door opening made her clutch her towel to her breasts. Dumb, considering he'd seen everything on her body many times over.

So she said her goodbyes to Carmen, then disconnected, going to the bathroom door.

The cowboy stood near the room's entrance, his hat pulled low over his brow. She could smell the cool of night on him, and it was just as quiver inducing as the pale of his eyes under his headgear.

Still playing the game—because that's all she had anymore—she gestured toward the tub. "I've been waiting for you. We've got tonight to ourselves before Carmen comes tomorrow morning to pick me up."

He didn't react to that news, perching his hands on his slim hips instead.

It didn't look as if he was in the mood to play.

He confirmed that when he spoke. "Back at dinner, I was sure that I could handle one more night. Just one, I kept telling myself, and then I wouldn't have to think about you anymore."

His straight talk put her defenses up full blast. "And…?"

"I don't know." His laugh serrated the air. "I have no idea about anything anymore. I thought I knew the rules, but they went and changed on me. That's why I told you my name and my place in life, because I was hoping they'd go different for you, too."

He didn't move, just kept his post by the door. The distance between them felt charged and thick, difficult to navigate.

But then he seemed to reject the atmosphere they'd created with their wounded, conflicting intentions.

"How old are you?" he asked gently. "Can you at least give me that?"

"Why?"

He whipped off his hat. "Because it's *something,* damn it.

And I've been walking around that parking lot screwing up the balls to venture a question that might not set you off."

How had this happened when she'd been so careful to avoid it?

But…her age. Did it matter so much if she could make him feel better?

"Almost thirty," she said, and the moment she did, it felt good. Strangely, sublimely good. "These past couple of days almost made me forget that my birthday is… I'm going to turn thirty the day after tomorrow."

She stopped herself from asking the same question of him, because she didn't want to know. She did, but she couldn't.

Yet at her openness, he held the hat in front of him, gentleman style, his gaze going soft.

She'd messed up. Oh, God, why had she told him?

"Just in case you're wondering," he said softly, "I'm thirty-four." He took a step closer. "I like quiet nights watching the night cover the sky. I like scotch and old cars and Johnny Cash. And my last name is Gray, from my family who's lived in Fielding, Texas, since before the Civil War."

When he stopped, the only sound was their breathing. Matched. Linked in a way that confused her and excited her and scared her half to death.

Then, slowly, as if he didn't want to chase her off, he reached out to take a lock of her hair between his fingers.

"And you, miss? What more can you tell me?"

Without him having to say it, she knew this was her last chance. This was the perfect time for her to risk everything, just as Carmen had told her to.

But it was also the perfect time to stay safe.

The longer her decision stretched, the more his eyes

dimmed. She realized that hope had been shining there, but it was too late. She'd waited too long.

He backed away, holding up his hands. Then, without a word, he donned his hat and pulled it over his eyes, shutting her out in the darkness that had first attracted her.

"Don't wait up for me," he said, opening the door and walking out.

There was only a click to signify that he'd fully shut the door, but it sounded like something breaking.

He'd left, just as she'd expected him to. But at least he'd done it before seeing all of the real her.

Their liaison hadn't been meant to last anyway, she thought, taking off her towel and going to her bag to change into something that would cover her up more. So why be sad?

Parting had been inevitable.

After she'd dressed in a short nightie, she crawled into the wide, empty bed in the awful darkness, hearing the click of the door over and over, replaying the moment he had left.

The sound of something breaking…

By the time her eyes grew weary of looking at the ceiling and finally fell shut, she had figured out what that breaking sound was.

Her heart.

11

NEAR MIDNIGHT, Carmen stood in front of the sink, washing her face before hitting the sack. After checking in, she'd hopped into bed gear, too: an overlarge Social Distortion T-shirt that covered a pair of men's boxers—an article of clothing she found perfect for lounging, no matter who they were made for.

As she dried off with a hand towel, she took a deep breath then blew it out.

Just go over to Eddie's room, she thought, glancing in the direction of the adjoining door. *He's proven himself to be a considerate guy, so what's stopping you?*

But that wasn't really the question, was it?

Carmen tossed the towel to the counter. Instead, she should be wondering if she was entirely comfortable with a guy who treated her well but didn't share squat about himself.

Standing there wouldn't give her any answers, so she walked over to the door, hearing the mumble of Eddie's TV through the wood. The immediate sound probably meant that his own adjoining door was open, welcoming her if she chose to turn the knob and step over the threshold.

When they arrived, she had checked into her own room before the issue of spending the night together had even come up. It had been a preemptive strike, allowing her to make the ultimate decision tonight. And from the knowing look on

Eddie's face as they'd walked out of the motel's office, he'd known just what she was up to.

But he hadn't complained. It wasn't his style.

She laid her hand flat against the door, heart jackhammering as if to chisel away all her doubts.

Why not go for it like Lucy had done? Carmen kept thinking. Why could her friend do it but not her?

Forcing herself to get over the theatrics, Carmen knocked, then swung the door partway open, waiting for Eddie to answer before coming all the way in.

"You still up and about?" she asked.

"For you? Always."

She peered around the door to find him still dressed in a T-shirt and jeans, sitting in a corner chair with one ankle casually resting on his thigh. He put down the road map he'd been scanning, his grin at full wattage, inviting her to walk all the way in.

Buh-bang, buh-bang…

Her pulse wouldn't calm itself down. She would even bet he could see her heart pounding through her T-shirt, like in a surreal cartoon.

"Did you end up talking to Lucy?" he asked.

"No, it's too late to bug her." Carmen had seen the cowboy's truck a few doors down, so she didn't feel as rushed to find her friend now. "Tomorrow will be soon enough. Her man's going home, and that'll be the end of things."

An end. Carmen's time with Eddie might be over, too. Maybe this was the last night she'd ever see him. Maybe this was her last chance to do what her body was suggesting with every throb, every shiver.

Eddie tossed the road map on a table, and they just looked at each other. Carmen's belly went hot and tight.

She sure wished she had that old redhead, punk-girl confidence now. But…what if it had never even existed? Maybe being Malcolm's girlfriend in college had sheltered her from all the anxiety and doubt that dating brought on a girl.

Had losing Malcolm—her significant other, no, her *crutch*—made her this insecure?

Another thought gave her pause. What if being here with Eddie was her way of seeking that shelter again—if only temporarily?

On TV, a late-night movie provided thankful noise. Cops and bad guys. Gunshots and yelling.

Finally, she laughed at the tension, making Eddie do the same.

"You'd think I've never been alone in a room with a guy," she said. "This is ridiculous."

"Too bad I make you nervous."

"I'm not…" She'd been about to deny her anxiety, but she would be lying.

"I was hoping you'd come through that door." Eddie leaned his forearms on his thighs, lowering his chin as he gazed at her.

He seemed so young right now, and so alone without his group in the background. His camera stood on the table, and Carmen wondered if it was a better companion than the people he traveled with.

"Eddie," she said, sitting on his bed. "What's really going on here?"

He knew exactly what she was talking about—she could see it in how he *didn't* answer, in how he fixed his gaze on the TV instead.

"We started out flirty," Carmen continued, "then ended up tonight in separate motel rooms."

"Not by my choice." He shrugged one shoulder. "On that first day, it seemed so easy. Too easy, maybe."

"And then I started blabbing about Malcolm. That probably heightened the romantic mood considerably. I probably scared you off."

"No, I understand everything you've said about trust, and believe me, I don't mean to be so secretive around you, Carmen. It's only that…"

Silence, except for the TV. She reached over to the nightstand and grasped the remote, lowering the volume and catching his full gaze again.

"It's only that," she finished for him, "you realized I wouldn't sleep with you unless I felt more comfortable?"

"That's part of it."

She traced a seam on the bedspread. "Why is it that I thought it'd be so much better to have sex with someone I didn't know? I don't even think it's possible for me."

"Not everyone can hop into bed with the first person who seems interested."

"Can you?"

She'd been compelled to ask. If she didn't get any answers about him tonight, she never would.

Eddie crooked an eyebrow, as if not wanting to cover this territory. It was to his credit that he ended up answering.

"I'm only a red-blooded American male." Then he smiled a little. "But I do have standards, and you meet each one of them."

Her heartbeat intensified, throwing every rhythm of her body off-kilter.

"Sounds like you're just trying to get me into bed now," she said.

"I'd do my best if I thought a seduction would work on you." Eddie pushed the hair back away from his face. "I mean, hell, here you are right now in a T-shirt and boxers, and I'm ready to explode like you're wearing lingerie."

She clasped the hem of her oversize T, bringing it away from her peaked nipples. Meanwhile, her blood simmered, as if his confession had lit a fuse, setting it to sizzling on its way to a bang.

Still, she didn't close the distance between them. Then again, neither did he.

Eddie was leaving the rest up to her, wasn't he?

Hell, was he wary of a rejection? He wanted her—he'd said so...

Then why was he leaving it in her hands?

She could venture a strong guess. Eddie was still hiding something, and maybe he'd started to feel guilty about that.

At her silence, he leaned back in the chair.

He wasn't going to clear anything between them, and she wouldn't force him to, either. Having him come clean on his own was the point.

After all, *she'd* been the one who'd found out about Malcolm's betrayal, and he'd admitted his wrongdoing only after she'd called him on it.

Not that she would've forgiven him if he'd only come to her first, but...speaking up *mattered.* It didn't make the humiliation any less painful, but it at least showed some character.

Eddie had been gauging her this whole time, and when he spoke, he sounded pensive. "This is about your boyfriend. Because he broke your heart."

"No, he broke my spirit." She'd blurted it out before even

thinking. "Or at least my ability to take people at their word. Problem is, Eddie, you haven't given me any words to go on. That's why I'm sitting a canyon away from you, and you know it. Don't be disingenuous."

"How else should I be?" He casually spread out his hands. "I didn't think we'd see each other after that one night, so there was no reason to tell you anything. I'm just as surprised as you must be about how things…went from there."

Buh-bang, buh-bang…

Her pulse was back to knocking her around.

"I didn't intend to like you so much, Carmen," he said softly.

Her heart lifted, then did a dive back to where it throbbed in her chest. She liked him, too. He seemed to know her better than anyone else in life, except maybe her best friend. "Like" actually didn't even cover it.

"After that first night," he said, "I suppose I deluded myself into thinking that if you formed a positive opinion about me before I told you anything, you might not run off."

She was floored. He thought that much of her? This near stranger? How? And in so little time?

Then again, she'd been attracted to him the moment she saw him, as well. But it was *only* an attraction, right?

How could it be anything more?

Carmen moved to the middle of the bed. "Just tell me, Eddie. What could be so bad?"

When he met her gaze, the sadness in his eyes nailed her.

"You don't recognize my name?" he asked.

Not a good start.

Kilpatrick. Eddie. Edward…

"No, I don't," she said.

He looked relieved, but only for a fleeting moment.

"Should I?" Carmen asked, already thinking that she should've left well enough alone.

The oxygen in her lungs had gone thin.

"My dad—" Eddie stopped, then started again, probably thinking there was no way to avoid this any longer. "My dad is Lawrence Kilpatrick. Assemblyman Kilpatrick."

A minivortex drilled Carmen between the eyes. Kilpatrick. She did know the name.

California State Legislature. A politician who was known as a bigot to some voters, such as her mother and her friends. Mama hated the man's guts.

Eddie was watching her closely again, and her reaction caused a rueful expression to take him over.

"Yup," he said, "as always. His name's enough to suck the air right out of a room."

She remembered on the houseboat, when she'd made him the *agua de melón* drink and explained how it'd been passed down from her Mexican relatives. He'd gotten that cautious look on his face that she hadn't fully read at the time.

But now it made sense.

She finally managed to speak. "Did you keep your silence and tell the rest of the group to do the same because you assumed that I disliked your dad? I'm not saying that I don't, but—"

"I don't make a practice of admitting I'm related to him. The minute a person knows that I'm the son of one of the biggest political lightning rods in the state, they tend to associate me with him. So I just shut up about it. The strategy has never failed me with people who aren't around for long—just as I thought you wouldn't be."

So Eddie hadn't wanted to lie to her, and that's the reason he'd never come out with the truth?

"Not that it matters now," he added, "but I don't usually agree with my dad, and he hates that."

She was still absorbing all of this. Assemblyman Kilpatrick. Yeah, her family would be *really* happy to know that she'd been hanging out with his spawn. Mama would flay her, and her normally easygoing dad would even ask Carmen what she was thinking.

But they didn't know Eddie.

God, what was she talking about? *She* still didn't even know him.

"That only explains a fraction of who you are," she said, pressing on, not wanting him to see the shock that had enveloped her. "There're still about a thousand more questions, like what's going on with the group you hang out with? And why do you almost seem separated from them?"

And curly, blond Trudy? she wondered. What about his strange dealings with that girl?

As if unwilling to see the fallout on Carmen's face, Eddie folded back the edge of his road map.

"How did I find myself on this trip with the brew crew?" he said, voice flat now. "That answer's easy. Trudy's my stepsister—"

Carmen blinked.

"And she roped me into coming," Eddie continued. "She was on dad-mandated probation after getting into some trouble at a bar. Just a kid being irresponsible, really. But she wanted to go somewhere on spring break, and she came up with this idea for Lake Havisu. Without asking me, she told Dad that I'd already agreed to come along and monitor her behavior—like I didn't have plans, myself. But I think he took great satisfaction in making that a condition of the trip. He made it clear that there was no way she would be able to hit the road if I didn't, knowing that I had already booked a trip to New Orleans for some picture taking. He also knew I wouldn't disappoint Trudy. Of course, *I* liked the fact that she had the gumption to outsmart him and get her way in the first place, so I canceled my other plans so her scheme would come to fruition."

"You'd do that for your stepsister?"

"Why not. Trudy and I fight like a cat and dog, but we face off against Dad together. Besides, I knew there'd be great pictures out here, too. Beautiful ones."

His green gaze swept over her, and she blushed, recalling the photos he'd taken of her yesterday.

Their kiss, her breasts in his hands and mouth…

Butterflies awakened in Carmen's belly, and she put her hand there, as if to contain them. "So you paid for the houseboat because…"

"Because Trudy's a disaster with money and she asked me to take care of everything and she would settle with me in the end. And she will. She just tends to do things like promise her pals that she'll spring for a houseboat if they come on the trip, so I'd rather curb that than have to deal with the consequences. She makes things harder than they need to be in general."

He paused, and Carmen could sense a "for instance" coming up.

She was right.

"Yesterday morning," he continued, "she made a call home and mentioned to her mom that I'd taken up with a nice girl named Carmen. Trudy didn't mean anything by it, but Dad got wind of the information, and you can guess how that went over in the Kilpatrick household."

Her pride took a hit. She wasn't all Mexican but enough to get angry about the implied reaction of his father.

Eddie had to have known how she was feeling, because he rushed on, as if to distance her from the reality of what he'd been keeping from her. It occurred to Carmen that he'd been doing more than protecting himself from a rejection.

Had he been protecting her, too?

When he continued, the answer became more obvious.

"I had a knock-down, drag-out fight with the old man over the phone and came back to tell Trudy to think about what she says to the parents from now on. I told her to be more aware of what comes out of her mouth, because she pretty much isn't. She was going to apologize to you, Carmen, but I told her to wait. It was only going to open a big can of worms, so I'm apologizing for all of this now."

"Eddie…"

"What? That's what you saw on the houseboat, the whole batch of dirty family laundry. I'm sure you were won over by it, too."

You had already won me, she wanted to say. But, no way. She couldn't go any further with this. It would be guaranteed trouble if Mama or anyone in her family ever found out—

She stopped herself. Was she living her life for *them?*

Eddie tore a bit of his map, his voice going lower, dredged with something that could've gone beyond pure lust and into…where? What?

"Women like you don't come around often," he said, "and I was going to keep seeing you as long as circumstances allowed it. But every day, we got further away from casual contact that didn't require me to tell you a thing. And now… Well, here we are."

He got out of his chair, sticking his hands into his pockets as his flop of sandy hair covered his brow again. This time, he kept hiding behind the long bangs, as if expecting that she would go back to her room now.

But her heart felt swollen, punched around. This had turned into more than a fling composed of physical desire.

"Eddie?" she asked.

He glanced at her, and there was something in his gaze so heart-wrenchingly obvious that she could barely look him in the eye.

"Can you also tell me that you aren't attracted to me because you know it'll piss your dad off?" she finished.

Because some ugly part of her got a twisted thrill from how *Mama* would react if she brought Eddie home. Did it do the same to him, too?

Not that it would ever happen. There was no future here. There was barely even a present.

He had paused in answering her question, and that told her everything.

Carmen sighed, and *that* seemed to say even more, because Eddie slowly sat back down in his chair.

"At first," he finally said, "it did appeal to me. I admit it, but now—"

"Now we should be happy that we didn't start anything up."

Once again, Eddie grabbed the road map, immersing himself in it as if it was another hiding place.

"Happy," he said, quietly mocking the word.

But, in spite of everything, she didn't leave. No, she merely turned the TV back up, refusing to go to her room, just wanting to stay with Eddie for as long as she could.

Because, with him around, she wouldn't be left alone with the knowledge that she might never have the courage to live her own life.

LONG BEFORE the official start of morning, Lucy had showered while the cowboy continued sleeping. Then she'd gone to the coffee shop for tea, which she took outside to a picnic bench near the rose garden.

There, she watched the sunrise, wondering if he was doing the same thing from their room's window.

An early mist burned away from the landscape, revealing more red and yellow petals on the rosebushes, plus the parking lot's damp blacktop. It must've rained at some point last night, but she'd never realized it.

Instead, she'd sheltered herself in a black sleep, not even knowing when the cowboy had come back into the room. But he obviously had, because she'd woken up to find him slumbering with his back to her.

Where had he gone? she wondered. And why had she ended up missing him so badly?

She knew the answer: because she had broken her *own* heart by pushing him away. But she'd done it for good reason. Survival. Safety.

Even so, those didn't seem like good enough reasons anymore…

Setting down her tea, she looked at the motel stationery she'd brought outside with her, then put pen to paper, thinking about what she would do from hereon out. The return to order calmed her, but only for a short time.

She couldn't organize her emotions. Not with the cowboy.

Joshua.

His name curled through her, somehow entwined with her now. She couldn't think about him leaving, of her going back to all her Lucy routines.

Why hadn't she stepped outside of her drawn-in lines to know him better? What could've happened if she had tried?

Footsteps sounded on the walkway, and she turned to find him, duffel bag in hand, his hat pulled low over his eyes, even though she could still see the pale of them.

They locked gazes for a thudding moment as the mist continued to lift, surrounding him in an ominous haze.

He dropped his duffel to the ground. "Time for me to go."

Numbly, she nodded, even though it was the last thing she wanted. But the leaving always happened. Always.

"You've got a lot of ground to cover before you get home," she managed to say.

"It'll be twice the fun with the amount of sleep I got." He fixed his gaze on the rosebushes. "All night I lay there wondering if you'd wake up. If I could apologize for walking out on you."

"No need for apology—"

"Yes, there is." He planted his hands on his hips. "I had no right to expect more."

Lucy's heart sank. See, he was accepting the status quo. He wasn't going to fight to stay, not as she had secretly hoped he would.

But a part of her wanted to do the fighting for them both. He'd touched her in a way no man ever had, and for a couple of days, she'd even thought there was something more in his eyes than lust.

Yet, that's why this was a good thing, him going. When she became something other than a playmate, he would see the real Lucy.

Let him drive away before that happens, she thought. *Let him go.*

Thing was, even if she was in control this time, his leaving hurt just as much anyway.

He kicked at the ground, as if wanting to say more.

"Joshua?" she asked, hardly realizing that she'd said his name.

But...oh, it felt nice. Truly liberating, making her sexual discoveries wan by comparison.

As he smiled slowly, joyfully, at the sound of her saying his name, Lucy's buried optimism rose up, crashing through the doubts.

Could she keep him here? Could she beat this farewell?

Suddenly, getting him to stay seemed like everything. It would mean she didn't have to go back to her old way of life, the existing and merely waiting for something better to come along.

She stood, stronger than she'd ever thought possible. "I'm thirty and on vacation, where my friend and I just wanted to feel better about the aftermath of our boyfriend breakups... until I met you." She ventured a step closer. "I work in human resources at Padme Software in San Diego, and my job bores me to tears. But I do like a good glass of amaretto over ice and movie marathons on Friday nights to help me unwind."

He'd taken off his hat by now, holding it in front of his chest.

She got even braver. "I don't let Carmen drive the car because I like to be in charge. I planned our whole trip down to the minute because I like...liked...to know where I'm going. And I don't...*didn't*...like any variation in the route, either."

"So why did you choose me?"

Her heart was about to crash through her chest. She couldn't tell him about the security of a stranger and how the idea tied in with the men who had disappointed her in the past. She couldn't tell him about the freshest wound, only a few months old, from a man who had seemed so right but had been pushed to the limits with her puppyish need for affection once a relationship had started.

But Joshua had a hopeful look on his face, and it was unlike any expression she'd ever seen him wear before. His gaze was softer, gentler, like light shining through a disappearing storm cloud.

She knew what he wanted, and she was finally ready to take a risk and give it.

No more strangers. No more games.

His knuckles whitened as he gripped his hat, as if in anticipation.

So she inhaled one more time, scared to death but diving in anyway.

"My name is Lucy," she said. "Lucy Christie."

Dropping his hat to his side, he laid a hand over his heart, then whispered, "Lucy," as if her name was his key to everything.

She just hoped it would be enough to keep him here.

LUCY.

The name was a burst of starry skies and sunshine all in one.

"Lucy" hearkened back to an age of innocence: lemonade on a humid day and root-beer candy from a sweets store's barrel, just as he'd first thought upon seeing her in that diner.

He'd been right about her, even back then. And he could easily picture her on his porch sipping that lemonade and enjoying sunsets with him.

"Lucy" was devil and angel in one.

"Lucy" was everything.

But just as he'd found her, it was time to go. There was no putting it off because his family was waiting back home, and it was his duty to stand up for them.

Joshua watched her awaiting his reaction, dawn cutting

through the mist to highlight her dark hair, to hush over the achingly vivid hues of her eyes and lips.

But not even the colors of morning could compete with Lucy.

He tried to find the words to convey how he was feeling, to tell her that he wished he could stay and that he would do anything if she would welcome him back another day.

Yet, at his silence, something significant seemed to strike her. Her shoulders looked as if they'd taken on a heavy burden, and the blue of her eyes faded a little.

What had just happened?

"I've got to go back to Texas—"

"Right, right," she interrupted. "Of course. Like you said, we knew this wasn't anything permanent."

Then, as if she'd donned another personality, she gave him one of her saucy smiles, transforming her from gentle Lucy back into the flippant woman who only required a good lay from him.

Joshua went empty. She was still playing with him, wasn't she?

Damn it, he was an idiot for thinking that the revelation of her name meant something more. He'd made it out to be such a big thing in his own head. But to her?

It was clearly just another teasing move.

The past few minutes hadn't been magic at all. Neither had the past few days.

He picked up his duffel, put on his Stetson low over his eyes so she couldn't read the profound disappointment in them. Then he tipped his hat to her and turned around to go his own way, a stranger once again.

"All the best to you, Lucy," he said.

"You, too…Joshua."

Her voice sounded gnarled, and he almost faced her again

to see if maybe he was wrong about her initiating another game. If she could possibly be feeling that there was a lot to lose here, too.

But he had to leave playtime behind now. People at home were depending on him, and he couldn't get any more drained by a woman who had just sucked a lot of the hope right out of him.

And, ironically, she'd given him most of that hope. Maybe it was fitting that she had the power to take it, too.

Joshua forced himself to walk away before he could find out for certain.

12

ANESTHETIZED, LUCY stared out the backseat window of Eddie's Cadillac as he drove them to Lake Havisu, where Lucy and Carmen's convertible was parked.

Everything was as stone silent as Lucy felt. Carmen and Eddie weren't talking in the front; they were only staring out their own windows while oldies music played on the radio, and that was fine by her, because Lucy didn't want to rehash the morning's events with Eddie around. She hadn't even gotten the opportunity to see Carmen alone yet, since she'd met her and Eddie at breakfast in the coffee shop and they'd taken off from there.

Besides, Lucy didn't want to put a damper on Carmen's fun. Talking could wait. Keeping her woes to herself was probably even a good thing, too, because it was hard enough trying to deal with the image of Joshua walking away, time and again, as she revisited it in her head.

She had revealed herself to him, and he had left. Why hadn't she learned from past experience?

Dwelling on it just made it worse, but she couldn't forget, either. So it was a relief when they reached the lake, where the Mustang waited in its parking space.

After apologizing again for the inconvenience she'd caused, then thanking Eddie for the ride and his efforts, Lucy left Carmen alone with him so they could make plans to meet again tonight. If Carmen came out of this trip happy, then it wouldn't be a complete heartbreak.

Lucy got settled in the driver's seat, catching a glimpse of the couple in her rearview mirror, noticing how they stood apart, how both of them had their arms crossed over their chests. Weird…

Finally, they hugged, and Lucy forced herself to look away.

Staring at the steering wheel… Holding back the sharp threat of tears… She wouldn't think about Joshua. Not now, not tomorrow.

It's just that, inside of her, he *hadn't* gone away.

Carmen returned, sliding into the passenger seat and closing the door. "Ready?"

"Yeah."

But truthfully, Lucy was pretty sure she would never be ready again.

She started the engine, nursing it for a minute, then driving toward the road. Eddie followed them, keeping a distance.

"Where're we going?" Lucy asked, thinking Carmen had plotted it out with Eddie. She didn't have the energy to care about their destination.

"I thought you might have an idea for our next stop," Carmen said.

Lucy shot her a quizzical glance.

Her friend didn't react, and that was when Lucy knew that the silence in the Caddy on the way back from Kingman had been more telling than she'd realized.

"You aren't meeting up with Eddie?" Lucy asked.

"No."

Jolted, Lucy pulled to the side of the road, and Eddie

passed them, his hand held out the window in a final farewell. Carmen watched, biting her bottom lip, until he faded into the distance, a part of the road they'd already traveled to get here.

"What happened?" Lucy asked, transferring all her emotion to Carmen's situation. It felt so much better to feel for her friend, not herself. "We have a lot of time left before we have to go home, so why aren't you seeing him again?"

"Because I never slept with him, Luce. I was too chicken to live up to my own dares."

Lucy didn't know what to say, so she touched Carmen's arm instead. "He dropped you because you wouldn't sleep with him?" she asked, just to clarify.

Carmen was shaking her head. "No, Eddie didn't drop me. I dropped him. I sabotaged any opportunities with him, and I did it because I'm a coward."

A car motored by, and the other woman's gaze followed it.

"You're not a coward," Lucy said. "Never have been and never will be. So you didn't sleep with him? No biggie."

"It's more than that. Even though it kills me to admit it, I just don't have the *cojones* to face up to the Ferris clan by bringing someone like Eddie home."

Right, Lucy thought. He wasn't approved by Mama.

"All the same," Carmen added, "maybe it was too soon after my breakup with Malcolm and I just need to get to know myself before I start up with another guy. Because that's one thing I learned, Luce—I can't sleep with a man unless it's going to be serious. My emotions get too tangled up in everything. It's just not for me."

Lucy thought about how it'd ended up not being for her, either.

She was rubbing Carmen's arm in sympathy, and her friend

reached up to grasp her hand. They didn't say anything for a moment, not until the other woman spoke again.

"I don't know why I'm so down about this." She took a deep breath and fluffed her hair, trying to seem carefree. "Let's be real—there was no future anyway. My family would've had a cow the second Eddie stepped through our door. He's Lawrence Kilpatrick's son, you know."

Lucy searched mentally for the name, wondering why that was such an issue.

But Carmen supplied all the rest, emphasizing the familial clash her and Eddie would've had—the politics, the headaches.

"Hardly a match made in heaven," Carmen concluded.

She'd raised her chin, and Lucy could tell she was fighting to convince herself that her vacation fling was nothing to mourn over.

But that's not what her friend's sorrowful gaze told Lucy.

"You're not even going to try with Eddie?" She felt her own sorrow creeping up on her.

Maybe she should've asked the same question before Joshua had gotten in his truck and driven off, leaving her standing by those rosebushes.

Carmen merely shook her head, and Lucy let it go.

Unfortunately, that left the subject of Joshua open, and as soon as her friend started asking about him, Lucy held up her hand, tears biting at her again.

"Later?" she said, swallowing. "But not now, Carm. I can't do it now."

Then, flipping on the radio, she eased back onto the road, having no idea where she was going.

Or where she would end up.

"MAKE A WISH!" Carmen said to Lucy over a week later as they sat at the bar in the Wine Cellar at the Rio Hotel.

The beige-bricked, low-lit ambience surrounded them while Lucy blew out the candle that stuck out of a slice of chocolate cake the staff had served especially for the birthday girl.

The crew behind the bar applauded along with Carmen, then went back to facilitating wine flights for the customers who were scattered at the bar and in plush, nook-enclosed lounge chairs.

"What did you wish for?" Carmen asked.

"That you would stop ordering me cake everyplace we go and remember that my birthday was several days ago."

Lucy grinned at her friend while giving her a fork to share the dessert.

But her smile died soon enough. It was hard to keep one going when all she could do was remember the many opportunities she'd missed on this near-finished trip.

Every day had been soaked in memories of Joshua, even as she and Carmen had continued on the Route, making it as far as the Texas border before turning around and coming back.

Although it was a big state, Lucy felt as if entering would bring back all the piercing thoughts of her cowboy that she had managed to tame.

At least somewhat. She found herself thinking of him whenever her mind wasn't engaged by road chatter or the stop offs where she and Carmen would busy themselves by learning Route history and culture. Every memory made her chest cave in, crushing her.

When they'd started back toward California, Carmen hadn't argued. She was just as ready to go home as Lucy.

Still, there were a lot of miles to cover, and while driving them Lucy revealed everything about Joshua to her friend. It hadn't helped much, not even when Carmen commiserated by talking about Eddie.

And this was probably the reason Carmen ordered so many cakes—because they could celebrate the fact that they were confiding in each other once more.

They shouldn't have ever become strangers, and they'd promised that it would never happen again.

After they'd finished their flights at the Wine Cellar, they did the Vegas thing: gambling, lounge showing, hanging out by the pool. It all seemed like marking time until they went back to the old life.

And, soon enough, the time did come for Carmen to be dropped off at her La Mesa apartment complex.

"Want some dinner?" the other woman asked as Lucy helped carry baggage to Carmen's door. The adobe courtyard boasted bougainvillea and Spanish tile, giving her friend's home a breezy, welcoming effect.

"Not hungry." Lucy patted her stomach. "I think I need to detox."

"Don't we both."

It was clear that Carmen wasn't talking about the greasy food or the many drinks. She was still thinking about Eddie.

"Just call him," Lucy said. "He lives in San Diego, too."

"Close yet so far away." Carmen stood in her doorway, as if reluctant to go in. "I'll call if you call Joshua."

Lucy's heart sank. "I…don't have his number."

"You have his license plates."

"And what will I do with those? Be a stalker?" Lucy started walking away. "He's probably on to the next conquest anyway. I won't flatter myself by thinking he's pining away for me."

"Luce." Carmen looked angry now. "Why do you say those kinds of things?"

Yeah, *why?* Hadn't she learned better?

She recalled how Joshua had looked at her, as if he did feel something beyond the desire they'd shared. How, if she'd accepted it, he might never have left.

"I talk like that," Lucy said, "because I'm in the habit."

Habits, schedules, itineraries… Hadn't she left those behind, too?

"Well, get out of it," Carmen said.

Then she tilted her head, as if coming to an epiphany, herself.

Had she made some kind of decision about what she needed to do, even beyond Eddie?

Or was this *about* Eddie?

The wistful gleam in her eyes remained, even as she continued telling Lucy what to do.

"You know where Joshua lives. Google him. Find him. Do something with him."

Lucy waved her friend off, promising to see Carmen soon, then heading home. But all the while she kept wondering if she *could* bring herself to follow her heart once again.

Once she arrived in her modest apartment, three blocks from Carmen's own, she unpacked, walked by her computer, unpacked some more, walked by her computer, ate a light dinner of ramen, walked by…

Crap. She finally turned on the darn thing.

She puttered around online, then started getting serious, finding a few references in a Texas online newspaper about a Gray family in Fielding, Texas. Obituaries for Mom and Dad, mentions of the horse-breeding facility.

All night she tortured herself with thoughts of him.

But she had to report to work the next day, and that gave her a reprieve.

At her desk, surrounded by all her organizers, Lucy mussed things up a little. A file left out here, a paper clip out of place there.

It was a start.

Then at the end of the day, after she'd lunched with co-workers, filling them in on the superficial details of her vacation as well as catching up on office matters, Lucy walked out of the one-story building and into the parking lot.

Intending to continue her search.

Maybe this time she would find an e-mail, a phone number…

She almost tripped when she saw a pickup in the lot. A red truck.

It was in better shape than the cowboy's, but the man reclining against its side was just as battered.

"Joshua?" she whispered, remembering how he'd shown up at Lake Havisu like this.

She closed her eyes, thinking that her mind was just playing tricks on her.

Yet when she opened her gaze again to find him standing away from the pickup, his hands clenched at his sides, she knew he was real.

Where the old, guarded Lucy would've walked toward him, this Lucy ran, dropping her workbag and coming to crash into his embrace.

With a groan, Joshua wrapped her up as if he'd never let her go, and she got dizzy with the lack of air, with the infusion of *him.*

He had come back, she thought, joy shooting through her.

He hadn't left after all.

JOSHUA BURIED his face in her hair, hardly believing he was with Lucy again, claiming her.

She was here, really here, and she had run to him.

He spoke against her ear, rushed and ecstatic. "I told myself to forget you. Kept saying over and over that I needed to put away what I'd come to feel and just concentrate on my purpose in life—setting wrongs back to rights for my family. It was supposed to make me feel better, make me a whole person again."

Lucy rained kisses over his neck, his jaw, then clasped his face between her hands and pressed her lips against his mouth, stealing his next words.

So soft, warm... He'd missed her, missed the future he might've had if he'd only listened to his heart and obeyed it.

She kissed him ferociously, hungrily, until he slumped back against the truck. His hands roamed her back, making all his dreams into a physical reality.

If he'd had any doubts about coming to find her, they were ash now.

Panting, she pulled back, her fingers tracing his lips, his cheeks, her gaze taking him in.

"And what about your business back home?" she asked.

"In progress."

As planned, he'd secured loans from old friends who would keep quiet until Joshua could approach Trent with an offer, but that wouldn't even be necessary. The community had indeed blacklisted the man, siding with Joshua. It was now even clear that Trent was trying to find a graceful way of settling this "land misunderstanding," and when Joshua got back, he knew the property would be his family's again.

He didn't mind making his neighbor sweat it out a little.

"But, Lucy, there was something about the way you looked when we said goodbye," he added. "Day by day, I couldn't forget that, and I missed you more and more. It kept me up at night, and nothing seemed as important, so I flew here, rented a truck and took a chance by coming to your workplace."

Her blue gaze went shiny, both with what he thought might be happiness as well as tears.

"I told myself that distance was going to cool your feelings," she said. "We live states away from each other and—"

"No." Joshua eased her hair away from her forehead. "You're the best I'll ever meet, Lucy Christie, and I'd be a fool to ignore what I came to feel for you."

The comment hung in the air, so he yanked it down, accepting the challenge of defining his emotions. "I want to know you, be with you, never leave you again."

She rested against him and started to laugh—a pure, relieved, exultant sound that vibrated his chest.

"Me, too," she said. "I was trying to look you up on the computer, Joshua. But you got to me first."

Inspired, he swept her into his arms, not knowing where he'd take her, as long as it was someplace private.

They looked at each other, too overcome by the passion that always melded them together. He wanted her, and he knew without a doubt that it was the same for Lucy.

But there would be more to come after they got their fill of each other. So much more.

"Head to the right," she whispered. "A conference room. Should be open. If not, I have keys."

She directed him toward an entrance on the outside of the brick building. It opened to an office with a long table, no windows, empty chairs, then another door that probably led to an inside entrance. He eyed it before laying her on that table.

There, he kissed her good and well, her knee rubbing against his hip, sparking him.

"I need to lock the doors," he said, bending down to kiss her again.

She *mmm*ed against his mouth before he broke away to secure the entrances, propping chairs under the knobs for insurance.

By the time he got back, she'd shucked off her suit jacket and tossed it to the ground along with her high-heeled sandals.

He took off his hat, as if out of sheer reverence for being with the woman he'd hungered for.

At his gesture, Lucy stopped unbuttoning her white shirt, looking as if her heart had caught in her throat.

"You're really here," she said, voice wobbly.

"And I should've been sooner."

"It's just…" She bit her bottom lip, shook her head. "Men don't usually chase me down like this."

His heart cracked a little at that. "I would've been a fool to leave you for good. Maybe I'm still a fool because I'm standing here across the room from you when I should be a lot closer."

She smiled, as if believing him when she'd never believed any other man before. It flooded him with the value he had been seeking—a near-impossible find that he had uncovered when he had least expected it.

"Joshua," she said.

His name on her lips was enough to make him shudder with ecstasy. An after burn roared over him, sensitizing his flesh with prickles of need.

She finished undoing her top, then allowed it to shimmy

down her arms while it exposed her pink lace bra. He could see her nipples through it, and the sight rocked him.

"Let me do the rest," he said, his steps eating up the distance between them.

He stood before her, taking hold of her legs and pulling her toward him. She slid on the table, then braced her hands on it while he undid her skirt with deliberate enjoyment.

"I have meetings in here, you know," she said, watching his every move.

He liked seeing where she worked. Human resources. An office. Just another facet of the woman who enthralled him.

"What would your coworkers do if they knew we were about to use this table for a more intense type of conference?" he asked.

"Forget work," she said. "Forget all of it."

A smile curved her beautiful mouth, and he thought that she had perhaps let go of something. Work? Or more?

She laughed, resting a hand on his chest. His heartbeat banged at her palm, as if separated by glass from her and trying to connect.

Pausing, she spread her fingers over him, seeming to link to the rhythm of his pulse.

Then she smiled again, and his heart tumbled to his belly.

"Let's get you out of these," she whispered, helping him out of his shirt, then unbuttoning his fly. His cock got anxious, blazing with a rush of blood.

She took off her bra, making a show of dropping it to the carpet. "Do you feel it?"

Yeah, he sure as hell did.

But she sent him a grin. "Not that. I'm talking about something else. This isn't how it was on the road. This is…"

She was leaning over to kiss him, and he understood what she was going to say.

This is how it'll be from now on.

She ended the kiss by running her tongue over his bottom lip, then saying, "I won't ever go back."

"Back to what?" He palmed her bare breasts, weighing the swell of them in his palms.

When he started kneading them, she closed her eyes.

"I won't go back to the way things were," she finally said. "I don't see how I can. Not after you."

She scooted toward him, bringing her sex against his, grinding and making him groan with the pressure of his need. But when she kissed him again, there was something else besides edged passion to it.

There was a softness, a sense of falling into a black, yawning hole, deeper and deeper.

He realized that only part of the sensation came from her pulling him down to the table with her.

Crawling onto the surface, he hovered over Lucy, caressing her face, grateful that he'd thrown caution to the wind and come to her.

They kissed gently, sucking with lazy draws. He felt her hands at the base of his spine, her palms slipping into his gaping jeans to cup his ass.

Another groan escaped from him as she nailed upward, abrading his cheeks, then sliding down again to push the denim away from his hips.

He reached down at the same time, taking out his penis, which had gone agonizingly stiff. Moisture beaded its head, slicking onto her thigh as he nudged it.

Her slight mewl signaled that she wanted more, so Joshua

allowed himself to prod her between the legs, her panties already drenched.

He could feel her cleft, and he ran his tip through it, painting her with his come.

In reaction, she squeezed his ass, then dipped her fingers between his thighs, touching his balls. He bucked, sucking air between his teeth.

Pushed to the limit, he yanked at her panties, ripping them until they uncovered her sex. She gasped, arching a little.

"I'm on the Pill," she said.

He didn't need a translation. "Lucy…"

Then he prodded her with his cock, almost collapsing with the pleasure of her slick lips against him.

He groaned. "Come home with me."

His words surprised him, but not as much as they did her.

She opened her mouth, but he kissed her to silence, his groin aching as he teased her with his erection, grinding against her clit until she whimpered.

"After you tell me your bedtime stories and I tell you mine," he said, kissing her behind the ear, "I could tuck you into bed every night and make sure you slept like an angel."

With that, he traced his tongue between her breasts, around each nipple, where he sucked and worked her around until she was squirming under him.

Then, he moved downward, over her stomach, her belly, her sex.

"Joshua," she cried out, wiggling her hips each time he used his tongue on her, *in* her.

But even as she pressed herself against his mouth, he knew he hadn't finished his explorations. No, he still had her thighs, every damp inch of them.

Behind her knees.

Her calves.

Her feet—the insteps, the toes.

Everywhere.

At this point she was in a quiet frenzy, one leg bent, one arm thrown over her face.

"My Lucy," he said, enjoying her erotic discomfort. It made him even harder, his cock pulsing.

Unable to hold back, he pulled himself up her body then drove into her, a primal cry coming from deep within at the feel of her closing in around him.

He moved his hips back, then rammed into her again.

Then again.

She took every buffeting motion with a moan, each one getting higher on a scale of notes that chipped away at him.

Harder.

Faster.

Sight going dark, he lost himself in her, crumbling away thrust by thrust. She was his rock, solidifying him even as she broke him apart.

He pounded into her again—another portion of him gone.

Again—another piece tumbled away.

Another...another...another...

Then—

Bang.

He blasted into the air, a freefall of dust spread to all corners of the room. A completion.

A completeness that felt like home and all its love and sunrises.

As he came to, he felt her stroking his hair as he rested his head on her breast.

Lucy.

At her touch, he began to build together again. Scrap by scrap, he formed into himself. A true man.

All hers.

"Joshua?" she asked.

Panting, he turned his head to see her. He smiled at her damp skin, her pink lips.

She smiled, too. "When do you need me to be packed?"

In spite of his weakened state, Joshua pulled her in for another kiss.

Epilogue

"LUCY!"

Carmen ran past her gathered relatives, past the beer keg, then past the food tables laden with tostadas, *carne asada,* tacos and all variety of offerings on her way to hug her best friend.

"You came," Carmen said into Lucy's ear as she held her tight.

Lucy drew back and looked at her friend, who was dressed for a late-spring family party in a pretty, light green dress. She'd let her hair grow out a little, but had kept it very red. Very Carmen.

"You wanted me here," Lucy said, "and I wouldn't miss it."

"Good. I'm afraid I'll never get to see you anymore, what with you being halfway across the country now."

"I'm never going to be far, Carm. Even if it's just a phone call away."

The two friends stared at each other, smiling. It'd only been a few weeks since Lucy had quit her job out of the blue then taken off for Texas with Joshua. So far, she'd discovered him by living in his cabin, and he'd done the same with her. They explored each other daily…and nightly.

But she wasn't afraid of what might happen if he found out too much. Not anymore.

She'd also helped him organize the papers for the deal

he'd struck with the ostracized Timothy Trent, and soon she'd be acting as more or less a manager for the Grays' oil business. There would be a lot to keep track of while Joshua and his attorney negotiated with a company called Tetra Research, among other parties.

Sure, she was still a routines girl, but she had redirected all that energy for a better cause now.

Carmen squeezed Lucy's shoulders. "You look so happy."

"I am. It's like we went on that trip for a reason, Carm, and Josh was it. He got me to like Johnny Cash—I had no idea how much I would—and I've introduced him to my mellow CD mixes, which I catch him sneaking into his truck."

At that moment, Joshua ambled through the patio door and out into the festivities, his cowboy hat lifted enough so that his face was clearly visible.

The handsome, gorgeous face that she couldn't get enough of.

Lucy watched him until he found her. Then it was as if her smile had struck a flame in him, and he glowed, smiling right back.

"Man on fire," Carmen uttered. "Can't get within ten feet of you two."

Before Lucy could answer, a little boy ran past her while escaping the outstretched hands of Mr. Ferris. Lucy laughed: Carmen's dad was playing monster with one of his grandchildren.

She thought of her own family. Her parents weren't altogether stoked that Lucy had left town, but they liked Joshua. Mom thought he was "delectable," which Lucy didn't even want to dwell on, especially since it had made her dad roll his eyes and grumble something she hadn't wanted to hear. But even her brother thought the cowboy was "good people," so she ultimately had their blessing.

She couldn't drag her gaze away from Joshua, who was accepting a beer from one of Carmen's pregnant sisters. Rita wasn't drinking—just serving.

Lucy forced herself to come back to the moment, and Carmen seemed to appreciate that.

"Okay, then," Lucy said, blushing at her own hopelessness. "Are *you* ready?"

Carmen exhaled, then nodded. "Ready as I'll ever be."

A voice broke into their conversation. "Ready for what?"

Both women turned to Mama, who was garbed in a polka-dotted dress. Slim, rosy skinned and poised, with her salt-and-pepper hair in a chignon, she reached out to hug Lucy.

"Look at our runaway," Mama said. "We miss your smile around here."

"Miss you, too, Mrs. Ferris."

The woman turned to Carmen. "I haven't seen Malcolm arrive yet."

Lucy willed all her strength to her best friend, and Carmen seemed to absorb it, her chin raised ever so slightly as she addressed her mother.

"Malcolm's not here," Carmen said, "because I disinvited him."

Mama didn't seem to understand. "*Mija,* why would you do that?"

Tell her, Carm, Lucy thought. *Just go for it this time.*

Much to Lucy's joy, her friend signaled to someone across the festivities, then faced her mom.

"Malcolm didn't deserve me. That's why, Mama. But I found someone who does."

Carmen held out her hand, welcoming Eddie into their circle.

His sandy hair was tamed today, slicked back carefully, as if for an important occasion. He was even dressed in a short-sleeved button-down and khakis.

Edward Kilpatrick meant business.

He took Carmen's hand and grinned confidently at her, then extended his other hand to the matriarch.

"Hello, Mrs. Ferris. I'm Eddie Kilpatrick. We met earlier."

Mama cocked her brow, shaking his hand but obviously on alert. "Yes, when I thought you were one of Carmen's many… friends."

"He's more," Carmen said.

Then she glanced up at Eddie, holding his hand in both of hers. A glint of what might've been more than just basic affection gleamed in her eyes.

In his, too.

It'd taken a few days, but after Lucy had reconciled with Joshua, Carmen had found the courage to call Eddie.

"I'd been telling myself to do it already, but you made me think it could actually work," her friend had said over the phone as she'd gotten ready for their first date. "As a grown woman who should be able to stand on her own, I had to follow my own advice for once."

And here Carmen and Eddie were, going public, with Mama looking as if she definitely had a few opinionated words about the situation.

Lucy could hardly wait until they told the older woman about Eddie's dad, but that would come later, after all the guests had gone home. Introducing Eddie now, in a casual setting, had been Carmen's way of taking baby steps, because she knew Mama would wage a war.

Yet, at the moment, Carmen was holding her ground, giving Mama a stubborn look of her own.

Lucy knew that her friend didn't need her immediate support anymore, so she wandered away, staying close just in case, then winking at Carmen.

She smiled as Mama started in on her.

"I see the fireworks have begun," Joshua said, coming over to put his arm around Lucy, then kiss her on the forehead.

She leaned her head against his chest, her heart sending off sparks.

"Definite fireworks," she said, wrapping her arms around his waist as they watched Carmen championing Eddie, the stranger who'd come to mean so much more.

And while Lucy's own stranger held her tightly, the fireworks kept on popping.

Lighting up any remainder of darkness.

* * * * *

Look for LAST WOLF WATCHING
by Rhyannon Byrd—the exciting conclusion
in the BLOODRUNNERS *miniseries*
from Silhouette Nocturne.

Follow Michaela and Brody on their fierce journey
to find the truth and face the demons from the past,
as they reach the heart of the battle between
the Runners and the rogues.

Here is a sneak preview of book three,
LAST WOLF WATCHING.

Michaela squinted, struggling to see through the impenetrable darkness. Everyone looked toward the Elders, but she knew Brody Carter still watched her. Michaela could feel the power of his gaze. Its heat. Its strength. And something that felt strangely like anger, though he had no reason to have any emotion toward her. Strangers from different worlds, brought together beneath the heavy silver moon on a night made for hell itself. That was their only connection.

The second she finished that thought, she knew it was a lie. But she couldn't deal with it now. Not tonight. Not when her whole world balanced on the edge of destruction.

Willing her backbone to keep her upright, Michaela Doucet focused on the towering blaze of a roaring bonfire that rose from the far side of the clearing, its orange flames burning with maniacal zeal against the inky black curtain of the night.

Many of the Lycans had already shifted into their preternatural shapes, their fur-covered bodies standing like monstrous shadows at the edges of the forest as they waited with restless expectancy for her brother.

Her nineteen-year-old brother, Max, had been attacked by a rogue werewolf—a Lycan who preyed upon humans for food. Max had been bitten in the attack, which meant he was no longer human, but a breed of creature that existed between the two worlds of man and beast, much like the Bloodrunners themselves.

The Elders parted, and two hulking shapes emerged from the trees. In their wolf forms, the Lycans stood over seven feet tall, their legs bent at an odd angle as they stalked forward. They each held a thick chain that had been wound around their inside wrists, the twin lengths leading back into the shadows. The Lycans had taken no more than a few steps when they jerked on the chains, and her brother appeared.

Bound like an animal.

Biting at her trembling lower lip, she glanced left, then right, surprised to see that others had joined her. Now the Bloodrunners and their family and friends stood as a united force against the Silvercrest pack, which had yet to accept the fact that something sinister was eating away at its foundation—something that would rip down the protective walls that separated their world from the humans'. It occurred to Michaela that loyalties were being announced tonight—a separation made between those who would stand with the Runners in their fight against the rogues and those who blindly supported the pack's refusal to face reality. But all she could focus on was her brother. Max looked so hurt…so terrified.

"Leave him alone," she screamed, her soft-soled, black

satin slip-ons struggling for purchase in the damp earth as she rushed toward Max, only to find herself lifted off the ground when a hard, heavily muscled arm clamped around her waist from behind, pulling her clear off her feet. "Damn it, let me down!" she snarled, unable to take her eyes off her brother as the golden-eyed Lycan kicked him.

Mindless with heartache and rage, Michaela clawed at the arm holding her, kicking her heels against whatever part of her captor's legs she could reach. "Stop it," a deep, husky voice grunted in her ear. "You're not helping him by losing it. I give you my word he'll survive the ceremony, but you have to keep it together."

"Nooooo!" she screamed, too hysterical to listen to reason. "You're monsters! All of you! Look what you've done to him! How dare you! *How dare you!*"

The arm tightened with a powerful flex of muscle, cinching her waist. Her breath sucked in on a sharp, wailing gasp.

"Shut up before you get both yourself and your brother killed. I will *not* let that happen. Do you understand me?" her captor growled, shaking her so hard that her teeth clicked together. "Do you understand me, Doucet?"

"Damn it," she cried, stricken as she watched one of the guards grab Max by his hair. Around them Lycans huffed and growled as they watched the spectacle, while others outright howled for the show to begin.

"That's enough!" the voice seethed in her ear. "They'll tear you apart before you even reach him, and I'll be damned if I'm going to stand here and watch you die."

Suddenly, through the haze of fear and agony and outrage in her mind, she finally recognized who'd caught her. *Brody*.

He held her in his arms, her body locked against his powerful form, her back to the burning heat of his chest. A low, keening sound of anguish tore through her, and her head dropped forward as hoarse sobs of pain ripped from her throat. "Let me go. I have to help him. *Please,*" she begged brokenly, knowing only that she needed to get to Max. "Let me go, Brody."

He muttered something against her hair, his breath warm against her scalp, and Michaela could have sworn it was a single word.... But she must have heard wrong. She was too upset. Too furious. Too terrified. She must be out of her mind.

Because it sounded as if he'd quietly snarled the word *never*.

COMING NEXT MONTH

#393 INDULGE ME Isabel Sharpe
Forbidden Fantasies
Darcy Wolf has three wild fantasies she's going to fulfill before she leaves town. But after seducing her hottie housepainter Tyler Houston, she might just have to put Fantasy #2 and Fantasy #3 on hold!

#394 NIGHTCAP Kathleen O'Reilly
Those Sexy O'Sullivans, Bk. 3
Sean O'Sullivan—watch out! Three former college girlfriends have just hatched a revenge plot on the world's most lovable womanizer. Cleo Hollings, in particular, is anxious to get started on her make-life-difficult-for-Sean plan. Only, she never guesses how difficult it will be for her when she starts sleeping with the enemy.

#395 UP CLOSE AND PERSONAL Joanne Rock
Who's impersonating sizzling sensuality guru Jessica Winslow? Rocco Easton is going undercover to find out. And he has to do it soon, because the identity thief is getting braver, pretending to be Jessica everywhere—even in his bed!

#396 A SEXY TIME OF IT Cara Summers
Extreme
Bookstore owner Neely Rafferty can't believe it when she realizes that the time-traveling she does in her dreams is actually real. And so, she soon discovers, is the sexy time-cop who's come to stop her. Max Gale arrives in 2008 with a job to do. And he'll do it, too—if Neely ever lets him out of her bed....

#397 FIRE IN THE BLOOD Kelley St. John
The Sexth Sense, Bk. 4
Chantalle Bedeau is being haunted by a particularly nasty ghost, and the only person who can help her is medium Tristan Vicknair. Sure, she hasn't seen him since their incredible one-night stand but what's the worst he can do—give her the best sex of her life again?

#398 HAVE MERCY Jo Leigh
Do Not Disturb
Pet concierge Mercy Jones has seen it all working at the exclusive Hush Hotel in Manhattan. But when sexy Will Desmond saunters in with his pooch she's shocked by the fantasies he generates. This is one man who could unleash the animal in Mercy!